T0064262

Love Affairs

Love Affairs

Arunachalam Kumar

PARTRIDGE
A Penguin Random House Company

To order additional copies of this book, contact
Partridge India
000 800 10062 62
orders.india@partridgepublishing.com

www.partridgepublishing.com/india

Contents

Preface

Love stories with twists and turns, this compilation of short tales, mostly inspired by true life incidents and events makes the reader want more: compellingly candid and almost real – the stories capture the core essence of romance. In a society deeply ingrained with traditions and conventions, to fall in love and end up marrying the one you love, is a rarity, too many socio-cultural mores and diktats make sure that love marriages are a rarity and often looked down upon.

The base for stories is set in a non-metropolitan south India: in this scenario, an alien one for those unfamiliar with the stringent and strict moral codes that define rural hinterland's man-woman relationships: to defy and defeat the elements stacked against genuine and true lovers is awesome and intimidating. This volume is dedicated to those that have succeeded in wedding the ones they wooed; May their tribe increase.

1

The fairy Godmother
and the princess

Once upon a time, long, long ago, there lived a young princess. She had all anyone could wish for. Beauty, riches, and a doting father, the King. Yet she was unhappy. She hadn't found anyone worthy of her. The King worried for his little daughter too, for, the suitors, all princes, were either too short, or ugly, or not manly enough. So every night she sobbed as she slept.

One night, a Fairy Godmother appeared in the Princesses chamber. 'Why are you weeping my child?' The princess then sighed and told her of her unfulfilled desire. 'A partner who would stay with her, and laugh with her, and sing with her, and who would love her'.

The Godmother waved a magic wand, and told the Princess. Never mind, we shall do something about this. She mumbled abracadabra, and then told the Princess, 'Before sunrise, go to the palace fish pond. There on the edge you will find an ugly warty toad. Gently pick it up, and kiss the frog. That's all you will need to do. The rest is my job, for I will reconvert the toad into a handsome virtuous Prince, for that was what he was earlier, before that witch cast a hex on him'.

The Princess was thrilled, and waited for dawn. She ran up to the pond, where, just as described she saw the most hideous looking amphibian there ever lived. Then, as she knelt down beside the toad, she was overcome with revulsion. She couldn't look at the fellow in the eye, let alone pick him up, and 'heavens be kind', plant a kiss on his slimy lips.

She ran back to her chamber, and sat and sobbed all day long. The Fairy Godmother came calling again. What happened? Where is the Prince?

The Princess then told the fairy of her situation, 'I just couldn't do that, kiss it, I mean', she sighed. 'It is so horrible and wet and sticky and slimy'

Dear, dear, the Godmother interrupted. Never mind, we shall do something about it.

Then she waved the magic wand, abracadabra she mumbled, and then disappeared.

The next morning every hand and page in the palace, nay kingdom searched far and wide for the Princess. She was found missing. The heartbroken king offered the kingdom's gold as reward, but none could ever find the Princess again.

If only they had searched thoroughly, they would have seen her. For Right here, in the palace pond, they would have found not one, but two toads. The Fairy Godmother had given the vain Princess all she had wished for, a partner who could stay with her, laugh with her, and sing with her, and who loved her.

2

Institutionalized infidelity

Certainly it must rank somewhere within in the top ten among the infidelity hot-spots in India. This little cool verdant niche hidden in the Blue Mountain valleys. My annual holidays, as part of my visit to a tea garden there, abutted this dubious village. The day was always busy time, tea pluckers, all women, moving about in groups deftly clipping off the tender twin shoots from the bonsai bushes of Camilla sinensis.

Come dusk, the twilight brings about a sea change in the serene scenario. Arguments, fisticuffs, screams, drunken brawls: the transformation into wildwest is total. The seemingly demure damsels that nary lifted their heads while picking the foliage, strut about in finery. They enjoy some edge, for on the plantations, women earn well, and regularly. The men are just drones, fit only to perform their daily manly duties.

The panchayat gatherings are stuff thrillers are made off. She ran off with so and so, he eloped with this one, and that vixen there seduced my man here, the charges are repetitive and ritualistic familiar.

One would scarce imagine a hamlet of this sparse population would be home to this many incidents of sexual indiscretions. Oh, that one, she got pregnant last year: and oh, this one's husband abandoned her for another.

I was witness to the sudden and unexpected death of the young Siva. He was an odd job man, fixing a fuse here, and a telephone there. Quite in demand on the estate where the bungalows often suffered electrical short circuits or blow outs. The remoteness of the estates meant waiting for days for the state electricity gang-men to attend to complaints. So Siva thrived. Always reeking of alcohol, he would shinny up any pole, and handle any hi-tension power line, with a devil may care panache. One day, full on scotch decanted by the estate boss, he hopped up the pole, and alas a fiery blast followed, and Siva tumbled down, charred beyond recognition. Pardon the inappropriate phrase: he got scotched, and got scorched. As usual, his death created ripples, with wails and sighs all over. Poor Siva, and so young too. Wonder what happens now to his new wife?

As his body was carried towards the hill edge for burial, the wife flailed her arms to the sky and beat her breasts quite pathetically. But her wailing ceased quite abruptly when she spotted another female from down the street, also wailing and flailing her arms skywards and beating her breasts. Boy was there a mother of all battles between wife and wench.

"Nee yaaraddi azhuvathukku? thayvidiyaponne... Kattinna ponjaadi naanu, azhuvudu neeya? ponadu en purushandi ..."

(Who are you to cry, you bitch. I am the wedded wife, and you doing the weeping?)

All the while poor Siva's body lay on the road, the pall bearers and attendant's all stood in a circle to watch the cats fight. God bless Siva.

Yet again I stood watching as the elders met to discuss how to deal with the elopement. Now this girl, just sixteen and just married was missing, and rumor had it that she'd run away to the plains to cuddle up with her paramour, leaving the shell shocked just wed groom, speechless. Then a good communicator was picked from among them to go over to the Nanjangud environs, and ferret out the lovey-dovey twosome, and drag the girl back, back to where she belonged. A kitty was raised, and passed on to the very determined looking scout that was drafted for the mission.

With no news about the missing couple or the one man posse sent out to rope them, the village folk were quite taken aback one day when they saw, the lover boy of Nanjangud, yes the very one who had hustled away with the week old bride, trudging up the hills. He shook his head and said, he had lost it all. What does that mean? Well you see that Kalliappa, the fox you sent to fetch Selvi back, well, he, ran away to Bangalore with her, leaving me penniless.

The last I saw was the two broken men, the contrite husband and the heartbroken lover, smoking beedis and drinking tea, exchanging notes. Truly, there is no place like this one for sheer drama. This small verdant hamlet tucked between Silver Oaks and tea bushes in the Nilgiris.

3

Love story: retold

His continued shaking his head for along long time, staring at the phone. Somehow he couldn't smother the smug smirk that took over. He reached across the table top, and turned the 'rip-one-page-per-day' book-calendar that was there. He suppressed the laughter that overpowered him, and ripped the 'yesterday' page. The new date stared at him now. 1st April. Ha ha, the all fools day. God, how Su had fallen like nine pins this time, after what she made me go through least year – just wait madam till you realize what today is, ha ha….Jay was absolutely delirious. Two years in running she had conned him – and made an ass out of him…but this time, this time…ha ha.

In ten minutes the phone tinkled to life.

Jay?

Su?

You moron! I hate you Jay!!!

Ha Ha, Su, but I had you didn't I? Ha Ha, what a con, boy I'll remember this for long girl…I can imagine your face…Ho Ho….

Jay you slime-ball, you sleaze-.. wait till I meet you. I'll make you pay lover boy. I really will…just you wait

Can't wait Su, can't wait….to see your sour face!!!

Meet you at seven after work, same place Jay.

Right madam, seven, and you won't believe what I've got for you Su, a diamond ring......you must see it.

Ring?

An engagement ring girl, and for the wedding that will follow. Su, the ring is so gorgeous.....

What engagement Jay? Who's wedding?

Ha Ha, Su, don't you try that stuff now, getting back to me for the April fooling are you? It will not work girl – not this year Su, in fact never again!!! At seven then, Su, Su? Sooo? Hello??

He tried calling up, but the line was dead. He was counting minutes for the seven date. The final date, today he'd slip the ring on her dainty finger, and call her Mrs. Su Jay.

At five minutes to seven he was at the usual rendezvous corner. The seconds ticked by. Seven, seven fifteen, eight. He stood waiting. He went to the telephone booth and rang

Su?

Yeah Jay?

What happened?

To what?

You're supposed to be here

Am I? So that I can be stood up eh? You nut. Once a year being fooled is asinine, but you think I'd let you do it to me twice in one day?

Hey Su, no serious, this time I am, I'm not April fooling around again this time, honest, believe me. And remember the ring, the diamond one, its waiting for you.

I already asked you in the morning Jay

What did you ask Su?

Who is that ring for?

You, my honeybunch, you Mrs. Su Jay…its got your name written on every facet, this piece of ice here.

But Jay, the problem here is…..

The phone got disconnected. He tried and tried, it stayed dead.

That night he slept fitfully: Did she really reject me? Is it real? Am I being shunted off? Booted? Or is it just Su's way of getting back to me? Am I being the biggest April Fool. Su always made me feel so, every April. He hoped it was so again. Or am I being told here is where the bus stops pal, go clear off? He didn't know the answers. He prayed it was all a joke. God Su! Are you serious? Did I go overboard in my plans, God!! What have I done?

And Su, she slept well that night. Deserves that, that Jay, she was smiling even in her sleep

4

Love story

She looked my way. I watch her. She blinked, I winked. She stifled a smile, I smothered an overpowering impulse. Total strangers, both. Just two in a teeming mass of humanity, but their eyes meet, and light up in recognition: they know, something tells them, they are meant to meet.

How uncanny and incredible this falling in love business is? The chances of coming across someone, in a crowd, who will in a few seconds make your heart thump and throb. Your nerves jump and jingle.

Is she alone? Does she have a boyfriend? Maybe not. I hope not. Maybe she has a wooer. Maybe he isn't up to her. Maybe she deserves better. I hope so.

Why did she look at me that way: the way only love can make one look. God! Am I the chosen one, am I better than him, I pray I am.

My heart flutters and fibrillates. A new surge of tingles course through my being. I smile again, to make certain. This time she smiles back, her eyes twinkling.

The bus stops. She gets off, and quickly walks away from my ken. The whole episode has lasted maybe six minutes, yet what an avalanche of emotions sweep over me. Love at first sight. Is this it?

I wish so.

There she is again today, in green today. Green? The 'Go ahead' color? Is it a clue? Am I crazy. Hey who is this with her, sitting right next to her. God! He is giggling and chuckling with her, telling her things which make her throw her head back and laugh. A steady, a suitor? Or just her brother? God, say it is so.

The bus stops and she gets off. He is staying back in the seat. He isn't getting down with her? Why? Aren't they in love? Are they?

I hate this guy. He is so detestable. So course. So crass. So gross. So undeserving.

There she is today, in blue today. The seat next to me is vacant. She sidles up the aisle. Hi! Her voice is like a Christmas bell. Hi, I reply. Can I sit here? Sure, sure. I wish I could scream sure, but I say it very muffled. Very politely. Hiding my emotions, throttling my desire. Biting my tongue.

Then, the bastard enters. Yes that unnamed rival of mine. My nemesis. She sees him.

Excuse me, she chimes, as he comes closer to us, 'hi, meet Ravi'. 'Hi', I mumble as she rises from her seat beside me, and goes over to the back of the bus with him to a vacant set of seats.

The bus stops. And I get down. I will walk the rest of the way now. I am a fool, an ass. For trusting my heart instead of my brain. How could anyone fall in love with a total stranger in a public bus?

Next day, they are both riding the same bus. Both nod at me. She leans over, giggles and says, Hi, did you know we met each other in this very bus?

And then Mr. and Mrs. Ravi coyly smile at each other.

5

Fairytale for adults

Did you sleep well last night princess

"Oh yes! Your Royal Highness, it was heavenly, the bedroom".

"Next", the Prince hollered.

He was now quite fed up with the endless procession of princesses who turned up to become his wife and future queen. He had one simple test. They had to sleep in a specially designed bedroom in his palace, on the luxurious and plush special mattress stuffed with the finest eiderdown. The Prince had secretly placed a pea under the mattress. And every time a new princess slept, he knew they weren't genuine, for they slept well, and said so in the morning.

How did last night go Princess? He asked the latest one to sleep in the palace.

Pooh! I didn't sleep a wink

Didn't sleep? The Prince asked incredulously, his heart trembling with anticipation.

How can a princess sleep on a bed like the one you have. It was so bumpy, I tossed and turned all night. My maid, who slept on the bed in her chambers said she slept well, but I, I just couldn't, something is wrong somewhere…

The Prince was overjoyed. He had at last found the perfect Princess, a fit queen for his kingdom. Only a real royal with cent per cent blue blood could be disturbed by a pea under fifteen inches of soft feathers that made up the bed mattress.

So he knelt down, and proposed. And she accepted.

The wedding was set for the morrow, all the kings and queens and royalty from every part of the country was invited. The festivity, festoons, fun and frolic. A royal wedding. The knights, the steeds, the footmen and golden carriages. Pomp and splendor. The "I do" was uttered with muted breath, under a giant-sized chandeliered church dome. You are now man and wife, the minister pronounced, and he kissed the bride as a token of his vow and commitment to the sanctity of marital canons.

Back at the palace after the day was done, the Prince, on his way to the royal chambers bumped into the Princess's maid and consort. He stopped to ask her if she was happy.

"Couldn't be happier M'lord" she said, "This is like a fairy tale. I just can't wait to go back to my country to tell my folks there how wonderful you and your people are, and how lucky my princess is!"

"Its time I told you my little secret", the princess said.

He had to tell this maid of the pea plan he had put into motion, and how so many royal lasses had been exposed as fakes. The Prince then told her of the pea under bed cushion trick.

"And I am lucky indeed, it does require someone of hi class and right breeding to discern the discomfort caused by a one single pea under the mattress"

"Oho" says the maid, "What pea?"

"The one I hid under the eiderdown"

"Oh no, my princess couldn't sleep, no matter how many inches of goose down you had there - not because of the pea, M'lord, but because of....

"But, because of? What?"

"Uh, er, er, mm" she fumbled for words. 'You see, her father, the King, was well aware of the flirtations of his daughter and her daily dalliances with the gallants of his palace, you know Prince how it is among the royalty - and so before he sent her here, he summoned the horrid blacksmith and had her fastened and padlocked with the meanest make chastity belt, and as you know M' Lord, who can ever can?,.....let alone a princess, ever sleep comfortably with that terrible cold steel contraption cutting into one's flesh?"

6

The surveillance report

"I want her tailed, for at least a month"

Jay was at the detective agency that provides private eye services for a fat fee.

A few forms were filled, and a thick wad of crisp currency notes were laid on the table as advance

It is time he had that gal Sue watched. She'd been acting up quite unusual and chirpy in the last few months, and something or someone was instigating change. He, needed to be sure, of her love, loyalty and fidelity. He had been till now. But of late, strange and morbid fears panicked his composure.

He dropped by at her shared apartment a few days later.

"Jay, I am so afraid nowadays, I think someone is stalking me"

"Tut tut, poppycock. Its your imagination".

"No Jay, I notice the Fiat every day, standing on the road across this room. Even my flat-mate Sheela noticed it. That car follows mine, to work or shopping, anywhere. In fact it just moved away before you dropped in".

Ha! Ha!!, he chuckled secretly. Good for her. Under surveillance, how does it feel Sue, big brother watching your every move. Curbs your style doesn't it. Hee! Hee!!. He feigned concern, and said,

"Just call me up Sue, if that jerk comes again. I'll take care of that cad".

He called every day, and yes, that guy was around again today, in fact he is here right now. So he drove up to her block, making sure he rang the dick's mobile en route. Just vamoose pal, is the message, vanish right now.

"She opened the curtain a wee bit", and said, "See there Jay… Oh my God, he just disappeared. He was here all morning".

Again and again, the ritual repeats, for days. The mysterious stalker just vanishes before Jay arrives to intervene. He rang up the next evening.

"Hey Sue, how are things going on, still being stalked?"

"Actually Jay, I have come to live to with it. Coming to think of it, it is like having a personal security guard, he is there everywhere I go. Makes me feel safe in a way, his presence. But I wish all this is a dream, and he will go away. Even Sheela is getting uncomfortable, and wants to move out".

"Sue, you need to see a shrink. You are getting persecution complex, and paranoid".

He was away for a couple of days on business, and on way back from the airport, dropped by at Sue's place. Time to check out things. He would call on the agency later, to get the dossier they promised – on Sue.

He knocked the door. Sheela was there.

"Jay?"

"Hi Sheels, where's Sue?"

"She didn't tell you?"

"Tell me what?"

"She had to rush to Bangalore. Remember that interview last month, she made it, and she had to report for her new job today itself. She left in a hurry yesterday. Bag and baggage"

Something doesn't gel here, he mused. He drove to the agency. He had to pay up the remaining fee, the four weeks surveillance report would be ready. He strode into the swanky office. The boss was there.

"Hullo Mr. Jay"

The bald headed owner of the set-up, gleefully collected the draft and handed over spiral- bind file.

"Every detail of every minute for a four week period."

"Thanks", Jay said, "and where is the detective who meticulously collated all this information? I must thank him too".

"Oh, he, that Sharan, he has been assigned a new case yesterday at Bangalore. He's good Mr. Jay, he handles single-lady cases exceptionally well, he has an uncanny knack that makes women trust him, and boy! He just loves Bangalore you know. I for one, suspect he has spirited someone very 'friendly' down there…he just resigned without notice…

7

The Sumitra is every married man's life

I felt an elbow nudge into my flank. I jolted awake, and looked at the bedside timepiece – 3. 35 A.M.

I turned over to see her, and noticed even in the dull glow of the night-lamp, her eyes was wide, and she was fully awake.

What did you say her name was?

Who?

That female you were talking to on our way to the market last evening

I don't recollect mention any name- and for God's sake it is three in the night

You did

Did what?

Mention any name?

I did not, any way if it is that important to for you to know it now, it happens to be Sumi

Sumi? I thought you said Sumitra?

Yeah, Sumitra, Sumi, its all the same

Is it? I thought Sumitra becomes Sumi only to the inner circle, I am a woman, I know.

Okay, you know everything. I'll dispose the twenty-two volume Encyclopedia Britannica tomorrow. Wife knows everything.

I turned over again, tucking my head inside of the blanket. It was chilly, and I needed some semblance of material cover from this midnight grilling session

I must have snoozed off rapidly, for I felt another jab spur me awake

You know her quite intimately don't you Mr. Romeo?

Know who?

That slut Sumitra, your Sumi

I switched the main lamp on and propped myself up on the pillow. Boy! She is serious. And she wants answers now. I knew it was coming, the innuendos, the insinuations, the works.

Shameless, that Sumi of yours

Of mine? From when?

You tell me Lothario, from when, how should I now? I just mind this house, rear the kids, cook, scrub, mop, sweep How can she stand there, right beside you squirming and oozing and wriggling like a worm on embers. She has the hots for you, sure about that, this Sumi. Who does she think she is, Simi Grewal?

Coming to think of it, that female did act quite coquettish and effervescent. She was all eyes, gestures and mannerisms, and all of them exaggerated too. But hots for me? Not Sumi. She was like this only, dropping her pallu at the drop of a hat, bending low exposing her prized cleavage, giggling at even flat jokes, and even winking wickedly – not with me, but with everyone else she was with.

Oh! She's quite harmless, Nam.

Don't you Nam Pam me? Just stick to my name, Namita.

Right then Mrs. Namita, Goodnight.

I leaned over and switched the lights off, and re-sheathed myself in the blanket. I felt her bend over and whisper

I'm sorry.

Me too, I'm sorry too

Twenty minutes later, I feel the elbow again

Now what?

You said sorry too

Yup I did

Sorry for what? Are you guilty of something you should be apologizing for?

Come into my parlor said the spider, aha - this one I married was quite a deadly Tarantula. Or maybe a Praying Mantis, the female of which species just decapitates her suitor and makes a meal of him.

Sorry I called you Nam instead of Namita.

Hmmm sigh! For a minute I presumed you were sorry for referring to Sumitra as Sumi. Never mind. Sigh. Goodnight. It is I that has to sweep, swop, scavenge, scrape, scrub....from dawn to dusk-------

Note: I do not know how it is with other couples, but I am certain dialogues such as the one here, are far more frequent, even in happy marriages, than is presumed. There are quite a few Sumitras around. As for Namitas, every wife is one. If you are a married man and say no, you must be newlywed, or lying. Just wait some years more friend. You will feel an elbow dig into your back and.........

8

An unusual love story

I rushed from the airport straight to her place. I had to meet her first thing – to express my condolences and, at the same time congratulate her – my old friend. I had been in sporadic contact with her while I was abroad. Note the odd combination of words, congratulations and condolences – yes, there is story behind their use here in a single sentence.

She had got married, an arranged one – but fate had other plans – within four days after the wedding, she was a widow. Cruel, kismet is. Her husband had committed suicide. Left a note blaming society. The worst part of becoming spouseless is, she discovered facing kith and kin. The note was signed by not one, but two. A woman too. A married woman at that. The suicide pact said, we cannot do without each other, and this is our only way out.

That hurt. She sobbed and wept, locking herself in her room for days. Why couldn't he be a man and say no to our marriage? Why mess my life. Why? The questions racked her sleep.

Terribly sorry to hear this Sumi. How could he?

Sumitra just stared at the floor awhile. *Life moves on,* she says, lifting the links of her mangalasutra. *I am at peace now.*

Mangalasutra? Do I see your eyebrows knit and rise? Yes, Sumitra remarried. That's where the congratulations bit comes in. You see, Sumi, was had always been the odd one. Bold, daring and unconventional. In six months after the tragic events that shook her life, she had found a caring man.

You must meet my husband Vijay. He is such a kind man. I am lucky, says Sumi, as Vijay walks in.

Congratulations Vijay. Sumi and you make such a matched pair.

He nods and smiles, *Sumitra is such a lovable woman. She is one of a kind*

So are you, so are you, Sumi interrupts.

I sit back and watch the couple. I am happy for Sumi. She deserves him and the happiness he brings into her life.

Vijay excuses himself and leaves. We, Sumi and I, get down to chatting, old friends, exchanging notes, sipping coffee.

How did you find him Sumi? It's hard these days to find any eligible groom, and to home in on one who is ready to marry a grieving widow, that takes guts. The society here...

Actually Shanti, he was right there when I needed him the most.

I cannot understand Sumi? Right there?

Yes Shanti - remember the suicide pact.

Yes?

Despite my personal grief after the tragedy, I managed to find the dead woman's husband. After all, he too must be going through this hell I was. We sobbed over the telephone, unable to articulate our emotions. Then, on a whim, I met him. Vijay.

The woman who committed suicide - one of the two that died for each other, unable to come to terms with their marriage or partners, was the first Mrs. Vijay Sharma ....

9

Smitha, the neighbourhood darling

There's always one in the neighborhood. Always, like a sore thumb: messing up lives of all other teens. Yes sir, the goody-goody types that politely greets every adult each time they pass by. The kind that maxes maths, and forever is first in the class. The sort that wins every quiz, debate or elocution competition. Nightmares, this ilk is.

Oh yes and they help mums with the housework, run errands for every auntie in the apartment block. Irons her own clothes, oils and braids her hair. Is forever clean and neat. Ever punctual. In free time, they don't turn on the TV to MTV but curl up with some notes for revision. God, I hate these kids.

Every mum in the block wants you to be like Smitha. If she can, why can't you? I just lie sprawled on the floor watching cartoons, and mum walks by looking through that window – just see her, what is she, fourteen, and watch her taking out the dried clothes from the line. The moral of the parable – the bottom line, you are no good. You are a failure. You are a write off. You are this, you are that. God! How I hate these smart Alec kids. So shweet, so correct. Angelic, cherubic. The teacher's pet.

You open the newspaper to read up the cricket scores, and mum walks by, as if on cue, maybe you should read the small article on philately Smitha has written for today's 'children's page'. Is there no end to this phase? How long does this impasse last? Doesn't that Smitha become older, ever? Maybe go to college and move into a hostel. The collective prayers of every normal teen in the area would have been answered. But even the Almighty above, has a soft spot for this mini nun in civvies.

One weekend, all changed. Smitha was missing. Frantic search parties, very sympathetic and shocked neighborhood. Cops murmuring into walkie-talkies, jeeps driving by with red lights. Though secretly all of us, the 'also rans' teens felt elated, we were a bit scared too. Rumors about kidnappers and mean gangs went the rounds. Agitated parents whispered to each other in small groups. Curfew was declared for all of us. Blast it! Even in her absence, this Smitha tormented us and wrecked our peace. Our Saturday kite contest was off, as was the gilli-thaand tourney with the Salai Street boys. All month we had honed our gilllis to needle sharpness – and this Smitha decides to get herself abducted. How absolutely sadistic.

In four days they found her. Holed up in a shack at Goa with a strapping young man. She had eloped, and chee chee, the aunties muttered, got married to an Anglo-Indian boy. The Smitha episode made significant changes in our life styles. Disciplinarian parents, who wanted nothing but the best from their progeny, readily compromised on their ideals. Thank God! Mrs. Seshadri proclaimed, my Vinodini may be fourteenth in her class, but normal. Imagine running away with a Christian boy – and did you hear, the police inspector told me that she had converted. Of course it was a scandal.

As for us, the ones with handicap (mental), we thoroughly enjoyed the new found tolerance for normal kids. Smitha, maybe Sandra now, wherever you be - Thanks for disappearing. For this Saturday's final, amma operated her kitchen arrival-manai, personally sharpening the bilateral ends of our prized gilli. And we heard Bala's mum actually helped him heat-mix and stir the fetid glue for preparing kite twine maanja - and Vicki's dad, the Circle Inspector, actually signed his son's report card with a tandem of red circles decorating its face, without a single comment.

10

Love story of another kind

Three years of love. Courting. Laughing with each other, talking about life, their friends and families. The movies, the long walks along the beach. The midnight drives, celebrating youth and romance. Boy, he really loved this girl. She had everything her wanted. Today is the day, he decided, I must ask her. This evening will be the right time. At dinner.

So they sat, talking in whispers under giant chandeliers of the five star place. Two adults, in love. Behaving line children. Giggling over each others jokes, silly and stupid though some were. The evening wears on. Then he swallows the lump in his throat, held her palm across the dining table

"Su, if I asked you to marry me, would you?"

He had uttered the words slowly and deliberately.

For a moment she looked stunned, taken aback at the unexpected suddenly of his proposal.

She looked at him glassily, like in a reverie, like she was in an euphoric state of nirvana. Then she looked down intently at the flooring and carpet, a long hard stare at nothing there. The slowly, and deliberately, she replied with a smile on her face,

"I need a little time to think thing over. I'm so confused right now, so sudden, all this"….

"That's okay sue, I'll wait a lifetime", he says, giving a gentle squeeze on her land, your worth a lifetime's wait…

That night he slept fitfully. He tossed and turned. Something nagged him, and he couldn't place it.

Then it hit him, how can she ask for time. From me. I love her, she knows that. She loves me, I know that. My mum dotes on her, and her parents adore me. We are both known to be steady, and in love, for years. I stood by her in times of need and she has too in mine. We just can't stay away from each other, even for a day or two, without meeting up or talking over the cell. The cards, the gifts exchanged, the presents, the birthdays…the parties. We are one in every way, except as a wedded pair. Yet she, looks away, and ponders over the question I asked, as if it was unexpected. How can it have been? It must have sounded natural, to expect a man to propose, after wooing and adoring each other for three long years?

The questions kept him awake. Is she putting on an act? Does she want him to cringe, and wait, and toss and turn for the answer? Creep to her door, crawl at her feet, kneel? God, how could Su even consider asking for time? If I'd been her, I'd have jumped from my table and hugged and screamed. I would have done so, had she asked me. I love her, and she loves me, so what's to wait for? What's the mental debate she must have before she decides to answer the expected question she had expected over the last few months to be popped at any time, on any day. The answer could have been a silent nod. Wordless. But his world would have been made.

He went to work as usual next day. His office phone rang in ten minutes.

"Jay, the answer is yes Jay, I will marry you", she gushes - giggling and breathless.

His heart leaps, and thumps. His head reels and swims. God...Su...

"Wow Su, that's great news. Now that you've answered my question, I am so relieved and so thrilled. But the question was different Su, I remember I said, - if I asked you to marry me, would you?"

"Jay"

"And now your answer is you would".

"Jay, not would, but will"

"The problem Su really is, the 'if' in that question Su. I really didn't ask you to marry me, I just enquired, IF I did, would you...

There was a deathly silence on the line. He gently placed the phone back in the cradle...deserves that, that Su. His looked at the phone, shook his head, and smiled.

11

Honeymooners

How can two adults sit on a public park bench, back to back, sending SMS to each other? They can, and laugh hysterically, giggle like stupid loons too: that is if they are the just married, coochie - coo, coo and bill types. Does the status of being newlywed somehow deduct a few points from one's IQ? Appears so, or else how can rationalize this – come with me to the Blue Mountains, a fav haunt of the honeymooners.

Watch this lovey - dovey pair from the plains as they chuckle and run around trees, now watch closer, look, see that fellow stalking them? He aint no stalker, he is a professional videographer, retained by the couple to record their amorous antics up the hills. Watch that fellow gallop behind the twosome laughing to himself and laughing all the way to the bank.

Times where when coy couples posed in studios, staid and serious for the man under the back cloak to click one B&W print for posterity. Newlyweds just went underground and emerged a week after, much honeymooned and pretending they'd just been visiting an ailing aunt. Honeymoons were private affairs. Marriages were sacred and called nuptials. They walked round fires, not run round trees. 'Sipping honey sitting under a full moon' was a deft definition my some one gave me for the term honeymoon.

Just trail that stud, feigning to be a bibliophile, he browses books on cryptic crossword puzzles at Higginbothams. Fawning beside him, lazily flipping pages of Filmfare is his very impressed new wife. Gawd, what a sham! What fakes!! What a phony!!! The whole Charring Cross is awash the vapors of exotic perfumes and after shaves and sprays. But I guess, as long as marriage remains a public confession of a private intention, anything goes.

Have fun kids, and Mr. Groom, make the best of this brief interlude: not too far away, the magical 'wows' will disappear and the true import of the marital 'vows' will hit home. Brace yourself for the inevitable. One fine day, you will wake up to uppittu for breakfast and come home to upma for dinner.

12

He, she and her

The magic isn't there anymore.

Magic isn't there? Is that all you have to say?

No, really much more than that. You've become cold, and I know this may devastate and hurt you, I've met this woman in my office who.....

Guessed as much, the way you've been playing truant of late – always finding alibis and excuses for staying over late at work. It had to give, didn't it? The lies, the flings, the secretive trysts. Well, maybe I've made the big mistake trusting you with my life. Its time to be adult and sensible about this mess. Lets sort it out like civilized people. Tomorrow, first thing we'll sort this out at the lawyer's. Divorce by mutual consent, that the clause we will file under – I've already talked it over – and if we sign jointly on the dotted line, in just one year from the morrow, you are free and so will I be. No exchanges, no washing linen, no money.

Right, that about sums up this year long farce we've been enacting. And I must add here, now that you're so organized and methodical about the split – I hate the perfume you wear. It drives me nuts, crazy. You practically bathe yourself in that stuff. The clothes, the bed, the bathroom and the whole goddamn house reeks of that sick perfume.

She looked out through the window, a tear springing in her eye. So that was his parting shot. Not a word of kindness, of remorse – the unfaithful cad. How much was promised, how little delivered. She waited for him to leave and held her wrists to her nose: she inhaled the fragrance of her favorite scent. It was divine. How can anyone fit for pigsties ever appreciate class? She bit her lip. Someone will have to pay for this, she swore.

In fourteen months he married gain. The ravishing raven-haired doll in his office. Honky dory. All tickety boo it was, the honeymoon. Every head turned at every beach in Goa. She had oomph, in oodles. And thank heavens, she wafted in a cloud of a delicate alluring fragrance that lingered and drove him crazy.

He walked in home, and felt his feet stumble. His head reeled. Honey, what is that funny smell around here?

What smell?

That one, he says, drawing a deep breath - Like some jaded out of date perfume, a smell that concentrated attar brings?

She laughs, you are parosmic or paranoid or both

No, it is so real he says, crushing her in his arms, never mind. But he was intrigued, he couldn't get that smell out of his system. The sickening fragrance that his former wife wore, day in day out for the twelve months she was his.

The same smell he sniffs, the very next week. Call me paranoid darling, he says, but I am sure that's the same fragrance again.

You must consult with an ENT. You need a nose job, he! He! she laughs, throwing her head back. Boy, she was beautiful.

That night he slept fitfully. It was getting to him, the infernal smell was on the pillow, the sheets, the sofa the toilet. Then it follows him, every day. Like some evil spirit the scent haunts: like his ex had cast a hex on her former husband and his home.

He leaves for an outstation assignment. He will miss this female. But, he will be relieved of breathing in hell. His home was now awash with smell. The smell he loathed. His work finishes in less than his planned four-day trip. He rushes home – and sneaks back into his apartment. She loves surprises. He'd haul her off her sofa and carry her to the bedroom – he clicks the door silently and tiptoes in. He doesn't find her in her usual seat, he nudges the bedroom door – and stands, his mouth agape.

On the bed, tumbling in the silken sheets he sees his wife, wrapped in the throes of passionate embrace – with his former wife. The couple looks up. The divorced woman looks at him and sniggers, a sneer on her face.

He now knew the source of the omnipresent fragrance.

I loved you, you loved her and now she loves me. She is beautiful Jay, too beautiful to be left for exclusive enjoyment of any one man. Funny world isn't it Jay, says his ex, leaning over to stroke her partners tresses.

His raven haired wife, props herself on the pillow – Jay, I'm moving out – moving over to be with my love, forever and ever. We'll just settle this in a civilized adult way. You know there is this 'divorce by mutual……

He reels and holds his head, the sickening fragrance filling his lungs – making him want to choke. As Shakespeare said it, hell hath no fury like a woman scorned. He felt bobbitized. Castrated. Leaving him for another man, he'd hate that - but for another woman? He clutched his hair and sank into the plush cushion of the sofa, and sobbed.

13

The lover boy who loved lying

His shift was over: sitting crouched over a screen and keyboard – trying to figure out what that blessed yankee was drawling over the headphones – eight hours of hell: that's what being a transcriptionist is. Robotic. Mechanical. Automatons. That's what this career made you – like spring wound wall clocks. The turnover of employees was phenomenal. Enlist, try, quit. Attrition was heavy in this hi-pressure business. Not many last the odd hours and demanding rigors of work. Yet he' stuck on, for want of anything better. Laid back. Too long had he been unemployed, getting his daily dose of admonishment from dad for not trying hard enough to contribute to, personally, to the family piggy bank.

He had a more compelling reason to stay put: the chicks, boy they were pretty. Flings, dalliances, and flirtations. He liked that fringe benefit. No strings, no bonds – this alone was worth the time.

Phew, move to the elevator – six floors down and done, for today. The whole of India was on holiday; Raksha bandhan, and he, he had to slog. No off day sir, its nose to the grind working your tail off.

Oh ho!!?? who's this dish? This one in hip hugging jeans and tank top standing in the lift. Long brown hair swept across her face and tumbling down – and look at 'em curves man – this is the kind Taj Mahal's are built for: Swoosh, the elevator dips – eight seconds all he had –

Hi!

Hi

New around here?

Been around

Haven't seen you though?

Uh huh

He sized her up – she was a sizzler all right

Both stepped out of the building and just as she was about to turn left – he asks

Going far? (Now for the uninitiated this 'going far' is a sure ice - breaker in Karnataka – yelli dhoorana?)

Kumarapark East

Ah, just the route I am taking (he lied: understandable), I can drop you

She paused, and he moved for the kill –

Just hold on here, er, er, Sumitra

Sumitra? Hee, hee, my name is Suparna

(round one to Mr. Suave)

He ran to the parking lot and zoomed in with his second-hand motorbike

Ooh! A bike? I love bike rides

Hop on Super!

Super?

Super, that's short for Suparna, and er, me Jay

Jay zipped her round Cubbon Park and every other park in the city. Stopping over on roadside vendors, for salted jignuts, for roasted corn – for bhel. They sat down and talked about life, work, and people. That boss of mine, he sure is atavistic

Atavistic?

Yeah, ever notice the hair sticking outta his ears? That's a sure sign of his animalistic origins from lower vertebrates – direct from the chimps, this guy is – ughs

She didn't reply, obviously new around the office – he had to clue her in on that slave driver –

The only thing he needs to complete the image of the ringmaster he is, is a whip.

She hardly talked – good, he liked them silent types. Less gossip.

He leaned over, 'psst, I have to let you in a secret – actually the hair-in-ear ringmaster is my dad. He insists I work my way up the ladder – learn the ropes. Rung by rung, that'll help me the day I take over – boy, complicated logic I tell'ya, sitting over millions, and I ride this junk to work. Bah! '(neat, this straight faced whopper – he could tell by the way her lips widened and eyes popped, she was impressed)

Round two to Mr. Suave.

'Dad? You are the CEO's son?? Oh, me God…why didn't ya?'

'Never mind, just forget it,' he says, waving his hand dismissively, as he chews a blade of grass sprawled on the lawns Lalbagh

Jay?

Yes Super

She reaches out to his hand.

Round three, round three to Mr. Suave

He feels her delicate fingers work on his palm and wrists – tickles, this. His eyes are closed as his head faces heavenwards, lying on his back.

Here, Jay, this is my gift for you, she says shaking him awake.

He stares at his right wrist. Knotted around the lower forearm was a pretty raakhi. Happy raksha bandhan bhaiyya!!

Bhaiyya? Brother, hey Super, what's going on?

Well, well Jay – maybe I should explain – that guy, yeah, the one with hair sticking out of his ears, the one you said was your pop, is my daddy too – so that makes us brother and sister right?

His head swims and he sees stars. One lie too many.

K.O. Knock Out. Kayo. Technical Knock Out. The winner is Super Suparna…the only daughter of the CEO, Nova Systems & Solutions, India's leading BPO and medical transcription service provider.

14

Why do pretty girls end up marrying ordinary guys?

Ever wondered how, the more pretty girls are always hitched up with the less handsome men? My own survey of the odd scenario reveals that eight out of ten beautiful women, actually hook up with or get married to men who are just passably handsome, and in many instances, very plain looking. The 'Adonis' types end up with Venuses only on movie and cinema screens; In real life, the princesses invariably pair with toads.

I myself am counted a toad, and am nicknamed 'cockroach'. Mainly because of my average in height, weight, colour and below average in looks department. Maybe too, because I am really an amphibian or arthropod in anthropomorphic form. Either way, the point is, much to the utter amazement (and often, utter consternation), the 'crow' look-alikes of my college end up with the 'swans' of the campus. The population of the bevy of beautiful belles that hover round plainsmen, amazes.

I have a possible explanation for dichotomous crow-swan coupling.

You see, the crows, know they are crows and the cockroaches know they are just that, insects; vermin and overlooked: They have nothing to lose anyway, so, they dare to send the valentine card, or the bunch of roses or tinkle a bell - to the prettiest in the city. Rejection they can take, they know they probably will be, but they never give up trying.

Now, for the swans, all decked and dolled up, enveloped in a cloud of perfume, eyelashes aflutter, stand in vain for the never-forthcoming Lochinvars in shining armour. Instead, they have a bunch of Sancho Panzas, strewing petals at their feet, making them feel heady. The crows are born courtiers and wooers. They will boldly walk up to Aishwarya, sitting alone yonder, to ask for a dance: all the while, the handsome smooth shaven Galahads, reeking of after-shave and dripping in gold necklace and bracelets, wait at the other end of the dance floor, and hesitate; Afraid of asking, for fear of being rebuffed. That is the key. They cannot take no for an answer, these macho types: their egos won't permit them to take risks. But the cockroach, he is ready in approach, open in his admiration and genuine in his motive-and lo! The crows get the crown.

Next time you see an ill-matched married pair, the male Corvus splendens (common crow) with arms of the female Pavo cristatis (pea fowl) draped around him, don't rant, just rationalize, and rue: it could have been you and her, instead it is her and 'it'. The hare always loses the race to the tortoise. So said Aesop.

And so say all of us, the Periplaneta americana (the roaches). Amen

15

Blogger Angel meets blogger Anchor

He / she was fun, and could communicate. She waited for isolation, then again and again she logged on – his comments on her blogs were so sensitive and genuine. Whoever he / she was invariably wrote a line or two – and with time, the two line entries became a wee bit longer and expansive. Obviously, the fellow blogger was a regular reader of her write-ups. Once or twice, the remarks made were so considerate – it lifted her spirits. Four months now, a comment on every piece – and she was a regular poster. She wrote about herself, her husband, her tensions, her scraps, her ambitions and her fears –all anonymously, hiding behind a neutral handle. No one knew who she was, no one would ever. She had been cautious to cover her tracks – and never replied to any personally directed mail or comment. Reacting to praise or panning, both are subtle give-aways of a kind. You reveal a bit of yourself every time you respond with emotion. She stayed off, scrupulously, from being provoked. She just bit her lip and clenched her fist in rage sometimes when negative feedback hurt her – no, cool, cool her mind says, just blog, ignore comments.

But this commentator, he / she was just so full of life, and positive. He emanated vibes. Its as if she knew him. She remembered the Roberta Flack number

I heard he sang a good song, I heard he had a style.
And so I came to see him to listen for a while.
And there he was this young boy, a stranger to my eyes.
I felt all flushed with fever, embarrassed by the crowd,
I felt he found my letters and read each one out loud.
I prayed that he would finish but he just kept right on ...
Strumming my pain with his fingers,
Singing my life with his words,
Killing me softly with his song,
Killing me softly with his song,
Telling my whole life with his words,
Killing me softly with his song ...
He sang as if he knew me in all my dark despair.
And then he looked right through me as if I wasn't there.
But he just came to singing, singing clear and strong.

She felt blue when the expected two liners didn't appear, but they did, late but certain. A word of cheer. Just as guarded as she was about her privacy, she respected this person's right to remain incognito – until, one fine day, after a spat with her husband – she dashed off a note sobbing about how hurting her husband had been lately. She received the most supportive letter she'd ever read. She wrote again, and again, pouring her heart out to the stranger on the line. Her mate's infidelities, his dalliances, his sadistic streak – his perennial suspicions about her character - The replies were always, hold on, life has its downs – but has ups too. The she did the unthinkable. Can I call you?

No, I'd rather be the stranger you know. Your guardian angel. Your alter ego. Your companion in distress and despair – No, I cannot and will not meet you – and she continued confiding, for weeks and weeks. She hardly blogged these days. She had time only to receive and reply mails from the ethereal correspondent.

She felt her fists clench. It took months for her to break her online benefactor down. She had to meet this character. One who had helped her cope. But the impasse stayed. It had become an obsession now. A neurosis. She had to meet the one that sustained and stood rock solid through her troubles and trials.

Then she got an SMS; how, or why she didn't know, she didn't care. Yes, you can meet me. After a flurry of exchanges and emails, she found herself traveling by cab. She couldn't believe the person who she was writing and messaging, stripping her soul out to, was actually now, in her own city. Was it a he, a she, who was it? this 'anchor' in her life – she couldn't wait

She knocked the door, the third one in the corridor in the star hotel. A stranger opens the door

Yes?

Anchor? she queries, citing the handle as familiar as her own name to her

No, I am not 'Anchor' but you must be Angel?

Right, Angel, that's me, where's Anchor?

Come in, he says, go right in, over to the other room inside, he says, leaving the room, shutting the door gently behind him as he stepped out.

She entered the ante-room of the suite – and stared, shell-shocked, stunned.

There sitting on the sofa was her 'Anchor'. Her husband a sinister grin spreading across his mean face

Ah! Angel, come in, come - we need to talk, talk a lot

16

The nerd I love

Here's the best red rose I could find – to the man I love, I pronounce, handing it over after kissing the flaming red petals. I am twenty-two, working for a decent company, drawing a good pay packet. I am passably pretty, and I love this chap. I've known him for two years now, he is doing his post graduate studies in physics – and if all goes as planned we should be hitched in another twelve months. We dote on each other – I, a diehard romantic, and he, dreamy absent minded lovable gentleman. No whispers in your ears, no cards on Valentine Day, no romantic trysts under park trees and no candlelit dinners in fancy restaurants. But, as I said – just munching fried jignuts sitting on a wall with him was enough for me. No holding hands, no pecks on cheeks –let alone on lips – yet, he was for me the Prince Charming. A bumbling beau.

Gee, thanks – he says, holding it close to his nose, 'smells so fresh'

Hey Su, did you know that the pledges and parleys made in the days of yore were called 'sub rosa', under the rose literally, to signify that which is being spoken is to kept under wraps?

Uh uh

He observes the bloom, hey Su, see how the petals in the flower are arranged in circles and rows that follow a very specific mathematical configuration?

I stared back

Ouch, he says, the sharp thorn under the sepals draws a spot of blood from his index.

He quickly stuffs the finger into his mouth and wets the tip

Ughs!!

What's ughs here doll, saliva is a mild antibiotic, and helps the healing process start immediately. Haven't you seen animals lick their wounds, it is nature's own antiseptic first aid

I dab the finger with my dainty hanky.

He takes it from me, forgets all about his finger, holds the two ends of the hanky in two hands and whirls it over and over again – and then, with a quick and sudden forward jerk releases one tip of the cloth forwards, simultaneously pulling the other tip back towards himself – snap, a cracking sound is created by the reflex whiplash action – That Su, the cracking sound is a sonic boom – when anything travels faster than the speed of sound, it produces a cracking snap.

Lets move into the shade, the sun's quite sharp out here, I said

Mmm, the sun, helios – Ra to the pharoas and Ravi to the rishis – hey, Su, did anyone ever tell you that when you see the sun, it actually isn't where you're seeing it – by the time the light from that inferno star reaches us, the sun itself has moved further off – in fact it has already traveled for seven minutes and it is no longer where it appears to be

I wonder how I can go on – this guy in my life, is so full of trivia and tidbits that conversation, that is normal, is impossible with him. Everything – is analyzed, rationalized and scientific. That's what perhaps makes him so different. He is like an innocent child exploring, like a speleologist not knowing what the next turn would expose. For his birthday, he wants a set of powerful magnets, last year he was delighted with the outsize glass pyramid I gave him, a perfect prism, he exults, producing a sun ray directed dazzle of seven colors across my face.

We sip a coke: and its physics again. The bubbles and froth wont form Su if the glass walls of the bottle are perfectly ground – microscopic irregularities on the surface trap and release the bubbles.

I pay the bill, he never has money. Just metal pieces and paper, currency is – here he says, take this, pressing an antique coin – reading aloud the inscription on its face – eight kaasu, it says – kaas Su is an antique coinage system of the Portuguese India. Worthless value then, it couldn't buy you half a seer of sugar, but today, this amalgam is worth a few thousands, if not lakhs – so, what money – it is ephemeral and eerie, metamorphs at will over time.

We walk in silence – I have to ask him. Jay, can we make it. You are so laid back and casual about everything – how can I trust you to take care of me and our future and family. It worries me you know, this attitude of yours: why cant you try to be like others, at least for me. Sunitha says I'm making a huge mistake. I worry Jay, I really do. What about your career, can you earn, are you serious enough to want to? Or will it be like this, talking about prisms, pyramids and Pythogoras. We need a capital, a corpus, at least when we start. I've saved up around fifty grand – time you qualified and took up a paying job by early next year.

He looked sullen and depressed. His hands juggled idly in his jean pockets.

His eyes light up and his face breaks into a sunny grin – Su, I have a hundred and eighty six of these at home he says, shoving the Portuguese antique eight kaas copper coin into my palm. Each worth a fortune – a king's ransom.

I shake my head, this guy is a geek all right and a nerd – but what a lovable nerd. I'd marry him even if he was penniless. he is already busy chucking a flat pebble across the large rain water puddle - if you throw it fast enough, it will bounce off the surface Su, here watch, he says as he flings the stone on the water body - it jumps and hops and continues on the surface like a yo yo. Actually, he says, if anyone could move as fast as the pebble on the water surface, he could technically walk on water.

I wanted to tell him, Jay, being in love makes me walk in air, but he'd take off on a tangent again. I just shut my eyes and prayed.

17

The whole world loves
a lover, or does it?

Amidst whimpers, she lisped, 'please sir, they'll kill me –
just save me'……please. She said this in a very low quivering
voice as I knelt close to examine her injuries. Something
snapped in me. I was livid. I stood up and faced the boor
of a brother, who was red eyed and smelling of alcohol. For
the first time in years, I let loose a tandem of four letter
words – much to his surprise. I turned around and told the
parents and others gathered in a ring – I am sick of you. In
two minutes I could get a hundred students from the mens'
hostel and burn your house down. How dare you…

I was myself shaking with rage. I felt my wife's fingers
on my shoulder, calming me. I knelt down again to the
lump of live flesh on the floor. Wash yourself, get some
clothes and get ready. I am taking you with me. There was a
stunned silence as the girl limped off into another room and
returned in three minutes with a small bundle of clothes.
To the silent spectators, I said, this is the last time you will
see her here….

Then my wife walked her to the car and we drove up to the very hospital the battered doctor worked. She was admitted and put in cast and sutured.

Next morning a very contrite looking father gingerly comes to my place: inter alia, his version was they were very upset at their daughter's adamant stance vis a vis her marriage – and that had stimulated his son to go berserk. I heard him patiently, but mentioned that fortunately for him and his family, his daughter had not preferred not to press medicolegal charges and had given a history of an accidental fall as cause of the multiple injuries for the hospital records. Obviously, the man and his kith were frightened, and I pressed home, bringing the romance issue into conversation.

After a good hour of dialogue, he came around to accepting that he would wait for a full year, and if the lovers were as determined then as they were now, he'd nod. He solemnly swore he'd honor his pledge. She will be married to M.

I talked it over with the patient in the hospital. She was suspicious and said they are just playing for time sir, 'they will lynch me the moment you aren't around'. I re-assured her, it was a deal done in good faith, and that on her part she would stay off M for twelve months – then what? She queries. I will stand as a witness in the registrar's office and get you married.

I got her an additional post as Ladies Hostel warden and she was now eligible, by default, for subsidized messing and free lodging besides a honorarium.

A few weeks of silence, then the expected ensued. The brother was frequenting the hostel premises, sending anonymous messages and calls warning of dire consequences – return home, now, or....I got wind of the fear he was instilling in the already scared and scarred sister, and with some manipulation and machination, got her transferred to Manipal, a place 70 kilometers off, where our institute had a sister hospital. Leaving town or shifting elsewhere, were not options: M was still in his PG studies and she herself was bonded to serve the college for three years more as per her contract.

Even at Manipal, once too often the family harassed her through calls and once, performing some 'black magic tantras, at her staff quarters doors. She rang me to ask whether her mum was okay, apparently her brother had informed her to come post-haste as their mother was on death bed, seriously ill. It was obvious that this was not the spirit with which I had trusted them. I informed the Manipal police, who sent word to the family at Mangalore, to keep off from ever calling or visiting the town, ever. In effect they were externed.

That shut them up. I on my part, waited for the one-year hiatus to pass and found it was status quo. No way – not that boy – and never a meat eating Christian. Over my dead body.

That was that. I got my wife and her to visit Kerala, where she met with M's parents along with M. It was followed in a fortnight a church wedding. The girl converted and forever gone from her forehead was the round red kum-kum bindi. I often wonder how much lovers give up for each other. For this girl, knowing her background and tutelage, the decision to convert must have been frightening and momentous. But, as they say, love is blind. Suffice to add, the couple is devoted to each other and has a lovely five-year old daughter to coo over now. Her family is still fumes periodically. More like a dormant volcano spewing smoke instead of lava.

With M finishing his PG course in dentistry, he and his orthopedic wife left India to make a new start to their star crossed affair and life. They are both now in UK, doing very well professionally. Not once in the last twelve years have they visited India.

Postscript: the parents and brothers I do bump into now and then – and when I was in a soup of personal problems, it mentioned here – they enquired of my welfare and asked me if I needed any help. We could send you vegetarian food everyday in a tiffin carrier, the mother said, seeing me walk out of a mediocre thaali meal restaurant where I boarded after I suddenly found myself homeless. The son who so terrorized the sister is no more, he died of alcohol induced cirrhosis last year.

18

The love letters I wrote

It was an unusual request: can I pen some love letters?

Scribing love letters? Sure, that's my forte – writing soppy sentimental sweet treacle dripping prose and poetry-Cupid inspires me. And moreover, I had a steady girlfriend back then. And since geographical space separated us, I had to take recourse to writing long winded letters to keep the embers glowing. In those days when I was wooing and serenading – my word output was astronomical. Much gibberish, but pages and pages of that. Remember though, trunk calls were expensive, emails were unknown, mobiles were non-existent. Love letter writing was a fine art for me. Embellished with sketches, caricatures and cartoons, I dare say, despite their being quite nonsensical (in retrospect) mine were readable. I still have here with me, a good many missives of mine, written in a frenzy in the seventies: re-reading them I am amazed how comical and ridiculous the contents were. But, as you all know, when in love even muck tastes like manna

Thus then, when Salim, a postgraduate student in the hostel – now engaged to be married to Jamila wanted to post a few lovey-dovey perfume dabbed amorous notes to his would be, I was enlisted as the ghost writer. It must be mentioned here that, despite perception, many medical students have pathetic talent for the written word. I have often heard terms such as cookers (for cooks) and 'suicided' among others used frequently. For me, coming from rigorous Convent educated English background, where Wren & Martin was Bible of sorts – and the years put in, in mastering the nuances of puns, gerunds, oxymorons – not to forget the range of adjective clauses, and applications of present imperfect tense – paraphrasing and précis writing came easy – and it wasn't any wonder that Salim, whose vocabulary was rather limited and lexicon, pleaded for sugared sweet-nothings in ink.

In next three months, I wrote many six to eight page long-winded pieces, all of which Salim faithfully re-wrote in his handwriting and posted –making certain that he dabbed a few droplets of his favorite (but dreadful) attar on the inside of the envelope.

Of course, he didn't show me the responses and replies, which by the frequency and volume of deliveries by the mailman, was quite astounding. I was also noticeable that the postman left a trail of a mystical smelling fragrance in his wake, no doubt, the leftover atmospheric traces from another 'favored' attar that Jamila had sprayed liberally in her envelopes.

Well, we all attended Salim's nikah at Bangalore. WE weren't able to have a dekho of the future Mrs. Salim, for as is customary, she along with her maids in serving was in another nether part of the choultry. Salim had made arrangements for a special lavish spread, mounds of spiced and scented biriyani and piles of colorful sweets. For me, in deference to my fastidious slavery to vegetarianism, a special corner table was set up, laid with the best in Bangalore could cater for grass eaters – a gamut of fare from MTR., served on a silver plate.

After the festivities and bonhomie, it was back to soporific medical texts. Pretty soon, Bangalore and its diversions was a distant dream. Salim, he came back after a fortnight's hiatus. He had brought his wife to Mangalore for a break and he invited me to say hi to her. I sat pillion on his Vespa scooter ride to Motimahal.

Meet Jamie, he says, and I extended my pal, noting that the bridal mehndi on her hands were still faintly visible

Jamie, this is my best pal, Kumar. Remember I had told you about him and his scrapes.

Oh yeah, Kumar. The guy who rode an elephant to college? Hi

We chatted for the next quarter hour, she was quite a good conversationalist – and her English was impeccable. Sophia's, not only teaches good English, but also trains its pupils to talk with a quaint imported accent. The dialogue soon turned around to more personal levels.

So how do you find this guy?

Oh, Salim!! He such a staid fellow. He, he, Always serious, hardly converses, just monosyllables. And he loves chicken teeka – wants it every day, breakfast, lunch, tea and dinner. Tell me Kumar, is that normal?

Salim smirks, smiles and butts in, "that's why I am arranging for a cooker"

Both of us blanched white. He meant cook. She shakes her head and mutters tsk tsk under her breath, leans over and whispers "and to imagine he can write such lovely letters – in flawless and flowery English. Real dichotomy this, Kumar. It's a mystery really, how can Salim can write so grammatically, romantically, yet be so clumsy in spoken English? You must read his pre-nuptial notes to me.......

Salim, frantically gestures to me from behind her: his index finger taps his lips - desperately.

I quickly rise, look at my watch – pretend I am late for something, say bye and vamoose. Salim stumbles behind me as I wend down the hotel's spiral staircase – phew, he says, catching up – close shave. He drops me back to the hostel, whistling the then popular Asha Bhosle number "purde mey rahne do, purda na utta-o"

Very apt, very appropriate.

19

Naughty notes from the Nilgiris

Shivakumar was an odd job man. Young, street smart and live wire – indeed, a real live wire. He was much in demand in the remote tea gardens and estates in Nilgiris for his genius at fixing electrical problems. He could shimmy up any pole to mend cables and power fuses. The frequency of outages and failures on the power front made him an indispensable one-man Mr. Fixit.

Not a day passed without some summoning him urgently. The few bungalows that the estate owners lived in were notorious for faulty lines and as we all know those that have lived a life of luxury, cannot do without umpteen electrical gadgets humming all day. Shivakumar, was their open sesame to lifestyle; keeping them in comfort lined his pockets well.

I often suspected that he himself had no small role in engineering mishaps – which judging by the frequency of their occurrence appeared, rather more man-made than mechanical. I saw the metamorphosis in personality too, from a checkered blue lungi he graduated to indigo blue denims. By virtue of his dashing hairstyle which was swept across his forehead and his expertise in flicking his Scissors cigarette from two feet off smack between his lips, a la Rajni

made him quite a hit among the nubile females who plucked
tea leaves – and despite his being wed, the cad had little
compunction in dalliances with the besotted.

Then jackpot! The bounder won a raffle in Ooty.
He become quite famous all over the hills after his snap
appeared in Thina Thanthi, a popular Tamil newspaper,
standing beside a shining Maruti 800 which he won on the
lottery ticket he had bought for 50 bucks. The blackguard
made a grand entry into the valley, tooting his car horn
(echoing all over the range). He was even spotted giving
a few giggling coy fans (females) a ride up and down the
winding slopes.

Behind every success is a woman, so goes the maxim.
Now, Mrs. Shivakumar, who got wind of the joy rides he
was offering to every petticoat, pavadai and pombalay- made
her next tactical move: It was I that gave him the money
for the winning ticket, she announced at the tea shed – and
that 'vandi' is mine, not his. Much muck and mud was flung
between the two, often in public. In fact the white Maruti
stood outside his one room abode for weeks as the war
waged on its ownership. The fellow even brought some estate
owners to pressurize his 'ponjaadi' to forsake her claims –
but she stood rock solid. My car, my ticket.

An uneasy calm followed the fracas – till one fine
morning, Shivakumar, accidentally touched a high tension
wire and was charred to death on the pole itself. His wife sold
the car and with the tidy packet, was much sought after –
and soon enough became one Mrs. Kadiresu: they invested
wisely, in Holsteins, which provided with a regular income
thanks to the Nilgiri Milk Producers Cooperative - rumors
have it some hanky panky is afoot here too, for Kadiresu is

the local secretary of the cooperative that doles out claims –
he promptly knocked off all the cows (clandestinely sold, the
grapevine has it) and pocketed a huge insurance return on
the stricken dead livestock.

20

How I wooed and married the girl I loved

She dotes dogs, the girl's father said. So, I did notice. She was all goo goo and ga ga over the half a dozen pooches that were all over her as she sat on the sofa opposite me. Me, twenty six, and in love – with this girl, who I discovered was more than crazy about canines. In the few months of courting and wooing I had heard her, now and then referred to one or other pooch: her reference to the mutts as him or her instead of the usual it should have alerted my antennas, but it didn't – I thought the anthropomorphic allusions were cute. That's what being in love does. One is so besotted by voice or looks that one doesn't hear what's spoken or see what's written (on the wall)

Now, those who know me, know me as one who cringes and shivers when dogs are around. They salivate all over you, they growl, bare teeth and despite my best behavior hold their tails very rigid and unmoved. I loved the girl, but, the package deal wasn't what I bargained for – love me, love my dogs.

I watched her, she was hardly even listening to her dad talking to me. For her, we just weren't even there. And she had her eyes, ears and hands for were the bounding and leaping and licking pets of hers.

Isn't he gorgeous?

I stiffened with pride, finally some references and footnotes on me.

You should have seen him when he was just a pup! He was adorable and choo chweet – he still is!!!

I deflated fast. This was getting nowhere.

I came back home and took a shower. I was smelling like a kennel. All night long I heard yips, yelps and yowls in my sleep. I looked around my apartment, a small two room affair. The very thought of six dogs prancing, racing, chasing and yapping gave me the creeps. God! I had to do something. I loved this girl.

I ruminated over the choices, Hobson's choices: it would be 'she and me,' it could be 'she', 'she, me and dogs', or it should be 'just me'. Though it fair broke my heart, the last option appeared the most rational and practical one. Well! I could give it one last shot. I picked up the phone and dialed.

Hi!!! said the voice at the other end, long time no see, no hear, no near: I heard shrill barks in the background.

Su, I have to tell ask you something

Sure, I'm waiting darling, just pop the question – the answer is ready, wow!

I heard it as bow, and stiffened.

Su, I hope you like cats?

Cats!???

Yup, Siamese cats.

Siamese what?

Cats. They are silvery golden regal pedigree felines with lustrous black eyes and sinuous swishing tails.

CATS! They are eeks, and their slow – mo tail twitches make me see red.

What about Manx cats? Ya like them?

Manx? What the heck is that?

Manx cats – they are from the Isle of Man, tail-less.

What? No tails! Is that an animal or what? Jay, what's this catty stuff suddenly?

Su, I have three cats at home, I lowered my voice and gently said prrrr purrr, very cat like the take off was.

Hey Jay, what's that funny sound?

What funny sound? (I said prrrr purrr again)

There, there! That eerie....

Oh, that's Julie, isn't she gorgeous? Actually she was so adorable and cho chweet as a kitten, she still is!! I planted a wet noisy kiss on the back of my hand.

You're bussing that thing?

What thing?

That CAT?

Who Julie? Hush, she doesn't like to told she is just a cat. She thinks she is human. I fact all three of them take exception to any references to a possible feline gene in their make-up - Hey! hey, scram, cut it out there, leave my socks alone – that I yelled for effect.

It is six years since we've been wed. All she said was she wanted me to get rid of the cats. And all I wanted was she move in without her dogs. We signed the dotted the in the sub-registrar's office. It took her months to adjust to a dog-less environ. For me, though, it was easy: in fact insanely easy.

21

The silent angel

She was fragile. Like crystal glass. The type of person Cinderella's lost slipper would fit perfect. Maybe nineteen. And I, a boyish sixteen, at an age when the first stirrings of fluctuating hormonal levels effect physique, psyche and perception. Every day, I would watch her as she daintily threaded her way past the road, a stone's throw away from my school. Boy, was she divine. Delicate. Gossamer. Like the down feather of a newly hatched chick. Tender. Stiffly starched laundered cotton sari, billowed on her slender frame. Like a gift, all wrapped up. A Nipponese geisha doll. An aquiline nose, alabaster skin. For the first time in my life, I was in love. Madly. With this ethereal wisp.

Silently I would watch her each morning; at eight, she would amble along the pavement of the busy road, pausing a minute, before crossing it. A large vermilion adorned the forehead, no lipstick, no make-up, a cataract of raven black mane neatly oiled and braided painstakingly... fresh, that was the word, absolutely fresh. Once or twice, when the traffic wasn't as infernally cacophonic as it usually was, I could even hear the faint tinkle her silver anklets produced as she tiptoed delicately. Like a ballet dancer, she sashayed with panache.

I had to do something. No, I must. Whatever that was that needed to be done, had to be done fast. But what? And how?

Just as the morning's sun lit up the nether end of the street, I saw her. Dewdrop fresh. In a pink sari today. Gulp... she was coming, closer. And she wasn't crossing the road at her usual spot. Still on my side of the road, and striding, jingle-jangle I could hear the anklet bells, heralding her approach. Then, she was there. Right there. I mean, right here. Upfront. In my face. She looked straight, her large liquid bovine eyes, embellished in homemade kaajal. This 'apsara' looked as gorgeous from up-close, as she did from afar. I just stood. Lost. Parched. Dehydrated. Then she looked down, at the small neatly stacked sheaf of books she had cradled within crossed forearms across her breasts... she rummaged through the pile... and handed me a single book. In a flash, she was off, the decibels of her tinkles ebbing. In less than a moment she was across the road, on the other pavement, and gone.

God! She was this close. I had even smelled her talcum powder, Remy... and jasmine, streams of which had cascaded from her crown. Intoxicating.

I shook myself from the spell that she had cast. Waking up from my trance I looked at the book she had given.

From the bookshelf of a local circulating library. A fifty-page 'romance' in serial sketch cartoon format. The type, the west produces in zillions. Tall dark handsome men, cooing and wooing blue-eyed blondes. I flip-scanned the pages, and shook the book. A love letter maybe? Perhaps an address... or a telephone number? Nothing. Just a much-thumbed, dog-eared book. But just holding it felt good. It carried the fragrance of Remy. The title on the multi-colored cover read 'Because I Love You'. God! What a nitwit I was. This was the message -- the title said it all. She was in love too, and with me!

Next day, I was up at daybreak, and rushed out to the road junction. Waiting for eight, and her. Like a dew-sprinkled primrose she came striding down, her large eyes glinting in the sun's golden glow. This time I was ready. Neatly tucked into the book, I had placed a love note, with a sketch of two hearts, Cupid's arrow pinning them together. She was here now. I smiled, she smiled. God! Mona Lisa clone. Then summoning all my nerve... I asked, "What is your name?"

She didn't answer. She just un-flexed her right elbow from its permanent perch across her small breasts, and stretched it over towards me. On the smooth fragile unblemished skin of the forearm, written in capital letters, the alphabets MEERA. In indelible green ink. Tattooed.

She lifted her index finger to her lips, shook her pretty head side to side, and gestured... I cannot talk, or hear. A deaf-mute. I stood mortified. Shell shocked. Speechless. Dumbstruck.

God... she couldn't even hear the little tinkles of those little silver bells on her anklets. What irony of fate is this that makes one ripple angelic knells around, yet deafens the maker of those dulcet tones? The book stayed in my hands, shaking. She looked wide-eyed at my mortified look... shook her head ever so slightly, then turned away.

My heart broke; thirty-eight years after these events, it remains broken. I wonder why she never walked down that road again. The alluring fragrances of jasmine and Remy linger in my subconscious. What happened to Meera, I know not. I never saw her again. The book, with its tender love, undelivered. She never could hear me whisper, "I love you," or articulate those three words herself... but read, she can... and if ever she reads this ode, déjà vu could bring back memories, of when one abashed schoolboy stood shaken, shocked and speechless...

That boy, Meera, still aches for you

22

The love affair

Love is blind: of that there is little doubt. The truth of the tenet was driven home to me when, as a young tutor demonstrator in my medical college, I was privy to an unusual affair. My pay was quite pathetic (that it still is, is another matter). I had to look after a wife and run a home – both of which were far beyond my limited budget. Luckily, the landlady who rented me out a small place – took a fancy to my wretched existence, by cutting down the rent by half, and buying me with the other half, every month, an item or two for my sparse household. A water filter, a grinding stone and iron box - however, more than my woebegone life, think, it was my dog Pickles that got her fancy and favor.

She absolutely adored the mixed mongrel – for who, she even constructed a solid cement kennel with 'Pickles' embossed on its door. She would forever feed the mutt with one thing or other, a piece of chocolate cake, a cream wafer, a saucer of milk – and he being my dog, she had perforce to also, by default, pass me some goodies now and then. Pickles, though a genetic conundrum, was an excellent learner soon mastering a host of commands. He could sit, shake hands, roll over, bark or attack when asked. In fact he pooch was quite popular in the neighborhood, for he was trained to trot to the local store-grocery, with a basket in his jaws, bringing back a loaf of bread or some such item. The curly tailed fellow could also yank the long hemp rope used to draw pitchers of water from the well – a practice that won him much munch-able manna from the asthmatic landlady. His criminal record ran long: his offences, though were exclusive, in that he simply grabbed and tore apart any hen or rooster that dared strut from the Shetian hen coop, on the compound wall that ran separating our house from the Shetians.

Poultry possessiveness is only exceeded by the fixation for coconuts in middle class India. It wasn't easy paying for a dead and macerated chicken or two each month with my wages – and too boot, I was a vegetarian too – so Pickles usually ended up gorging on the leghorns, affectionately marinated, masala-ad or grilled by my landlady. On retrospect, I now think Pickles knew the succulent layers would be on his menu if he plucked them from the wall, a habit that cost me much. This tale though, is not about canine IQ, but about a love affair that scandalized the lane.

Just behind the row of houses stood the medical college boys hostel. Incessant growling and restless barking by Pickles late at night, made me wonder if anyone was afoot in the area. I tiptoed to the door and released Pickles from his corner. Woof, woof he yells, running straight behind the Shetian residence, where, he flushed out a very terrified medical student – who looks so ashen and pale in the beam of the torchlight I had – I feared for his well being.

Now what the hell is going on? I thundered, the decibel and din had by now awoken the whole neighborhood – Pickles could petrify anyone through his bark alone, let alone his bite. The student, a final year fellow named Suresh stood mum, unable to speak. I flashed the torch beam about, and anon, a female emerges from the dark shadows in the narrow corridor. What the bloody hell is this?

This is Benedicta – the maid who works for and stays with the Shetians. Mrs. Shetian was livid: known even in normal circumstance to be a loudmouth, she truly was in her elements tonight. The gist of her plaint, I soon gathered was, not so much the coochi cooing and cuddling that was going on in her backyard, but that it was so tough to get maid servants these days. She screamed at the shivering medico, you know how hard it is to find a woman to work? Find one for me before you drop in across the wall - you @#$$##**&&&&^%%. As I feared she would assault him in her rage, I quickly bundled off the shaking student to my house, where later, he told me that he was madly and totally in love with Benny (for Benedicta).

The boy must have been twenty-two at most, and Benny was at least thirty-three plus. Besides this, the ramification of the affair cut across so many bars, barriers and bans – I shook my head and told Suresh he was nuts.

He looks at the floor and asks my wife a very, very strange question.

Madam, have you seen Kokila?

Kokila? The Kamalahasan Tamil movie?

His eyes light up,

Yes, yes, you saw how the hero gets involved with a maid and finally marries her. This is just like that, Benny and me…

I sat shut and sickened; Heavens, my mind screams, give me a break, please. Save me from this numbskull and nincompoop.

By next morning Benny was packed off to her hometown, Mrs. Shetian cussing loud and long as she smacked her soaped wash-clothes with rage and vigor on the granite stone. In a week everything became quiet. Pickles slept well and even snored. Suresh, the medico vacated the hostel voluntarily and loved into a lodge room.

Eight years later, I was on my Rajdoot Bobby bike, shopping at the market with my wife, when a Fiat stops near me…

Hi sir, says Dr. Suresh, leaning over the driver's seat. On his lap is a little kid;

My son sir – Shailesh

He leans back to let me see the other passenger beside him,

You know my wife sir, don't you?

Sitting there is a beaming and a radiantly content Mrs. Benedicta Suresh

Daktarey, encha ulleroo?

She asks, and without waiting for an acknowledgement or answer continues,

Namma Pickle encha undu? (how is our Pickles?)

As I said right at the start, love is blind – but in a way I felt happy for this couple. They broke the odds and took on the world – and won.

23

He loved the librarian more

She took his breath away: each time he went to the consulate library, pretending to thumb voluminous tomes in preparation for the score in the ranking exams he was to take – score well, and you could find yourself back in this building on another queue – for a visa – and passport to greenbacks. But who can concentrate with this pretty thing at the counter – phew, a stunner, this library assistant. Ready toothy smile, twinkling eyes – hour glass figure and a dress sense that complemented her personality. She disturbed him, her presence. He had enrolled in the library as a member only to while away time – he wasn't serious about leaving shore.

A steady government job, a middle class home and loving family – a scooter maybe – his ambitions were modest, but peer and parental pressure wanted him to at least give the tests a go: thus he found himself here, in this bibliophiles Mecca. And what he didn't find in the books, he found here in the form of this angel – inspiration. No, not to read, but to be a regular user.

He watched her at work, glancing sideways – an overpowering urge to walk up and splutter out what his heart was telling him – grab her and squeeze her – but, hold it, he didn't even know her name.

Excuse me madam, I want to borrow this book

Right, she says, entering the details of the loan on a computer and giving him a counterfoil printout.

Seven days at a time sir, she tinkles with a radiant flash of her teeth, thank you.

Boy, he wished he could borrow every book on display, one after another just to be able to hear and see her up close.

He returned the book early, once again to be in proximity of the apsara – this time he left a small note for her inside the book: who knows, she may yet…

The following days, he fair ran to the library, but she went about her work as before. No sign of acknowledgement: no clue, no signal. He flipped every book he borrowed, tuned every single page in desperation, for the elusive reply note. But, the books were empty. Just the same "seven days at a time sir" accompanied with that absolutely disarming smile.

Then one day, as he shook the book, an envelope tumbled out. A wedding invite. He read it again and again. Sumitra! her name and she was getting hooked. His heart broke. He read again, no; not getting hitched to a blighter named Ajay – but already wed. The invitation was three years old. She's been wed for years? He sighed, silently, this was cruel, unfair – just the girl he wanted as his, was someone else's.

The attraction stayed. His admiration for her persisted. He continued visiting the library. Borrowing books, nodding a g'morning or g'bye now and then. So what if she was Mrs. XY or Z. She was a woman, and she deserved respect – and he was, despite his mental turmoil, dignified and decent fellow. Though the sock on his jaw and hurt, he maintained his poise and demeanor. He couldn't blame her, he could only rue his kismet. Not a word was spoken, two adults, behaving like two adults.

Four months later, a newspaper clipping slipped out of the borrowed book. He read the item. An obituary insertion. A grieving young wife and her little son paying homage to a young husband and father. It was dedicated to Ajay Sharma, and inserted by Sumitra, his wife and Sunil their son. A yellowing clipping from The Hindu, dated December 2001. It was October 2nd 2004 today.

A widow? How unjust life is? How punishing kismet can become? How could fate let this young woman to cope alone with life with a tiny fatherless toddler to raise? Alone? Why alone? Is there no way out? Cannot the machinations of karma be countered? Yes, if he made bold for a future and she made a break from her past. He does not borrow books or visit the library anymore. She brings home any book he needs. He is still unemployed, but he is occupied. Looking after a toddler is a full time job.

24

Invitation to a non-event

Then, there was this guy, Balasingam from Singapore. He was head over heals with that doe-eyed Bengali female in the class. In fact he attended lectures only to be able to sit on the bench behind her, watching her the whole hour. She probably knew Bala's fixation, but chose to ignore him – at least pretended to – for no matter what, most nubile girls need attention. He was like her puppy dog and she treated him like one – a dog. But strange logic governs romance, even when it is one way. Bala never gave up, she never gave in. Stalemate. Two years long the state of affairs continued. He religiously visited Udupi Sri Krishna Temple and a host of other places, sanctified spots; rumour had it that he'd even crossed the state border, into Kerala, where, he met with a black-magic practitioner for some hex and mantra that could turn the tide in his favor. He wore 'blessed' talismans and elephant hair bracelet – all to no avail.

His buddies saw he was heading nowhere, but who in love listens to those that aren't in? Till, one smart Alec whipped up what seemed a super scheme. He went to a hand-cranked printing press in Mulki, and with a couple of donors that sponsored the plan partially, got a wedding invitation ready. In a few days, he and his foursome gang, posted a hundred and fifty invitation cards to all and sundry, including to all teachers and administrators in the college, plus, one turmeric-pinched four-cornered one to Calcutta. Not forgetting another, equally sacred looking one to Mr. & Mrs. Shanmugalingam of the lion city founded by Raffles

Then all four schemers vamoosed from the town for a week.

Chaos and confusion followed the receipt of the invites, frantic international trunk calls, telegrams…the lines to Kuala Lumpur were choked. Frenetic representatives of the Principal and the college management dropped into the hostels. Bala, he was clueless, and no matter how hard he protested or pleaded his innocence, everyone suspected he'd had eloped with and married the Bangla bomb.

Despite his pious remonstrations and pathetic pleas, the needle of suspicion never wavered from pointing direct to him. By now, the clique that had engineered the fiasco was traced, and confronted by the Principal – who had, with him the very livid and murderous looking parents from Bengal – its then that the mastermind came up with his next master move – actually sir, the two are secretly married, we only wanted the world to know….Mrs. Sen swooned. Mr. Sen reeled. But being amid doctors they were soon revived and restored.

The plotting guilty were all asked to wait outside, while a much animated debate and discussion, that took a hour, went on inside the chambers. The upshot of the prolonged discussion was, now that the damage is done, and the two are, as reports from reliable sources suggest, 'married'…we might as well arrange for an official acknowledgement and public reception of the union.

Two days later, a still shell shocked banga bahu – exchanged garlands in the college auditorium, with the rock band 'Hamstrings' (made up of medical students) strumming cacophonic chords. The Sens appeared resigned. And the Shanmugalingams sent their blessings – we heard they were over the moon too, when informed that the lass was a Bengali, Mr. Shanmugalingam was actually seen sporting moist eyes - in his own remote way, he ascribed all Bengalis to the Subhas Chandra Bose genetic lineage – and who is there in Malay peninsula who didn't know how that, Shanmugam's, grand uncle was in the INA – and had saluted the Netaji way back and had served in the I N A.

He rang up one Mr. Soans, owner of the pompous sounding Soans Photo Electric Studio of Mangalore to cover the event, in color (remember back then, videos weren't around and even snaps were B&W only – Soans was the first businessman to start the novelty of color photos and even he had to send the rolls to Kodak in Bombay for developing and printing)

Thus, on one rainy day in the sixties, Bella Sen found herself become Bella Balasingam. Needless to point out that, after this unusual hitch up and the circumstances that led to it, much suspicion and doubt was created whenever any wedding invitation card was received by anyone. For a few months more, all printed invites were double checked by recipients for veracity.

25

Two branches, two silver oaks

The air was biting chill, the intoxicating aroma of freshly distilled wintergreen filled my lungs. This is heaven, lost amidst the misty wisps and clouds that drift across the high verdant slopes and sholas of this secluded Shangri-la. The Nilgiris, the Blue Mountains. Jutting to seven thousand feet into the sky, a profusion of wild orchids and flowers carpet the dales – and yonder, neatly manicured and pruned acres upon acres of tea bushes. I pause, drawing in a long lungful of mountain air – the hills are steep –and I tire easy. City life has made me lazy. I pause under a silver oak and drink in the scene. A score of women, tea pickers are down the slope. I can hear bits and pieces of chatter and chuckles from the bevy of cheerful women as they mechanically go about their job.

I close my eyes as I lie down, stretched on my back. I hear a baby bawl. The shrill cat- like wail of an infant pierce the thin air. I squat, raising myself on my elbows and look around. Another hundred yards or so behind the huge boulder, I see a native cradle. This contraption is product of a genius mind. A simple length of cloth, tied at its two ends with a rope, and strung from a tree branch or beam. The baby is securely cocooned within the hanging drape of the pendulum, which is swung this way and that to lull the babe to sleep. Warm in its shell, shielded from the sharp draught, newborns and toddlers sleep for an eternity. All it needs is a gentle nudge of the hanging pendulum once awhile – and the mother can work uninterrupted or snatch her own forty winks from trials and torments of motherhood.

I sat quiet and watched the cloth strung baby wriggle and yell in its confined space, waah, waaah, louder and shriller. I looked all over again. Not a soul within sight, just one single baby strung from a tree, writhing like a caterpillar in distress. Except for the knot of women way down the slope, too animatedly and excitedly gossiping and working, not one was in hearing distance. I shook myself, rubbing my palms to generate some heat – it was really cold and walked up to the bawling baby twitching in its hammock. I spread the two halves of the enveloped inverted tent splaying apart the ropes. I saw the most heavenly sight a human eye can ever see. A tiny naked chocolate brown baby, with eyes wide open, a large black 'warding off evil eye' mark on its chin, shrieking to high heavens. It was so beautiful, the sight – despite the distress the baby was probably in, I stood transfixed, something is so heavenly about little defenseless babes that appeals to all humanity, universally. I cooed gently and brought the vents back to proximity and gently rocked the tattered cotton sari hammock...the bawls petered out and in three minutes or less, it was eerily quiet again.

I slowly walked away, backwards for a few steps, only to be confronted, on turning, by a score of eyes staring at me; the women had stopped their chores and looking in my direction – and put their palms across their mouths to eclipse and stifle giggles. One woman, a young undernourished one, scampered up the slope, still giggling as she came up.

Tanks ayya

I don't know what to say. Maybe seventeen and already a mother – and if my reading is right she was no man's wife, a widow. The tell-tale yellow cord these hill women sport so proudly, was absent from her scrawny neck.

She knew, I knew. These simple folks can read eyes and expressions. They are schooled by generations of living close with nature. They know when a snake is afoot, the birds are twittering agitatedly ayya – they know when the rains will come, the aalkaati kuruvi (Lapwing) calls incessantly ayya – the ants are running in frantic lines ayya, rain is around – the termite mounds are humming, unseasonal showers arriving…

Ingadaan setthaaru ayya veetukaraar (he died here ayya, my husband)

I stood quiet.

Thooku pottukittaru (he hanged himself), laatri kullukku payithiyyam ayya, ellam pochu..(lottery ticket mania, everything was gone)

I dipped into my pocket, found one single note of ten rupees only. I opened the hammock and placed the currency on the silent angel. Wish you luck junior, you'll need plenty of it.

The daily lottery is ruining lives among these folk: How can a government sponsor gambling? How can a government trade in liquor? Questions confound and confuse me.

I trudged back heavy hearted to home and hearth, a roaring fire was warming the grate.

Strange are the ironies of life, one tree's branch supports a budding life and lulls it to slumber by gently swaying in the breeze…and another tree's bough helps another life extinguish itself – to eternal sleep.

Two silver oaks, two ropes, two scripts…two endings - one story, the story of life.

26

The hotel receptionist

I

Tired after an eight hour bumpy road ride…I checked into this hotel at the city outskirts. That would help me avoid the incredibly voluminous morning traffic tomorrow – a big day for me. I will have to be at the TV studio by 9. 30 AM. I turn on the hot water faucet and out jets a stream of biting chilly water!!!! Brrrrr…this is a cold place, and cold water isn't too pleasant for a refreshing bath (at least for me)…I was blue literally by the time I was through and pretty livid too.

I stamp up to the reception counter and vent my steam……how could a hotel of this dimension and stature not have 24 hour hot water???

The lady receptionist tried to mollify my upset mood by offering a million excuses, none of which were either convincing or sane. My rage dissipated rapidly after the outburst and a steaming hot coffee. I sat in the lounge flipping through the day's newspapers. Something made me feel quite sick inside. What could this poor lady managing the counter do…the maintenance department was to blame, the management was the culprit – she too, like me, worked for somebody – unfortunately, unlike me, she was on the frontline, always. Trying to be pleasant, smiling, looking pretty all the time, hiding emotions. Irate customers, raving drunks, nitpicking diners….Taking the rap from all and sundry. For the lobby receptionist, the buck always stopped at her table.

I saw her picking up her things and leaving work. As she passed by, I stood up and said,

Sorry…..sorry for the temper tantrum

She smiled radiantly, and I continued 'I was really tired and…'

Never mind, it was our mistake…..we should be apologizing sir, not you'

She was not around early morning as I left for the studio. I returned after four hours, relieved that the mental tension about how the interview, in Kannada, (a language I have learnt by hearing it being spoken) went off better than I had expected.

I packed and wanted to leave as fast as I could, in eight hours, I could be back in Mangalore for a homemade supper and a good night's sleep. I just needed to pick up a few things my caretaker Lakshmi, had listed out as 'musts' for the kitchen. I left the hotel and ambled around the busy marketplace. Shopping over, and laden with one thousand things I'm sure were actually redundant in the kitchen…I stood at the wayside waiting to wave down a auto-rickshaw. Walking on the sidewalk, with a little four year old kid daughter was the receptionist.

I nodded and said, 'Holiday?'

Yes sir,

Your kid?

Yes, this is Nayana…

Nayana, you want an ice cream?

The child's face lit up and she tugged her mum's hand, which in unspoken kid lingo means, say yes mamma. We walked up to a ice cream parlor a few yards off and the kid slurped her chocobar with much relish and drool, as I and her mother talked. What she poured out, disturbed.

This was a battered house wife. Her no good husband abused and bashed her every night. A sot, who reeked of alcohol – a lech who grabbed every rupee she earned- a wastrel who lazed all day and boozed all night. She went on, and on, hoping for better times. He was her husband, and she'd married him for love, she said. The prop of a mangalsutra and a man in the house (no matter if he be a beast of a man) was social security in this big bad city. So she goes about, smiling at strangers in the hotel by day, and getting shoved, hurt and bad-mouthed come night.

The other side of society, she told me of, also disconcerted. She came from a scheduled caste background, she whispered across the table. The hotel is owned by a Lingayat (Veerashaiva) baron, and if he comes to know who I am, I will lose my job too, for her is quite obnoxiously caste conscious. The job pays well and she is allowed to lunch there and even has permission to pack a few items for her family.

Ice cream over, the mother - daughter duo trudge back into the road, back home. If one can call it one. The child, her cheeks still sticky and wet, says 'tata, uncle'.

Happy Woman's Day…I say, as my auto jerks off…

I return to the room, and in twenty five minutes am back on the westbound National Highway, heading home. All along the ride, my mind replays the conversation with the receptionist and recalls her pained face. The pathos and poignancy with which people play out their assigned roles in the drama of life. The script writer has goofed up. But deliver she must, the lines written for her. Wish you well, working woman…I hope someday you find peace and happiness… may your daughter be your strength and succor.

How was the interview? Lakshmi asks as soon as the air-conditioned Ford's window is lowered…. Oh. The interview, it was okay…

I had even forgotten the purpose of the visit to Bangalore. It had been such a huge occasion and gung ho affair for me, this invite to appear on a widely televised channel. Suddenly, all that seemed so trivial and insignificant. Lakshmi is perplexed, she expected me to gush excitedly about how I had used the correct word in Kannada for 'whales, for 'scratching' for 'physics' for 'corners' for 'angle'….yet, here I was lost and moody…

The moist eyes of a tragic heroine, the receptionist and the ice cream smeared face of a small girl haunted and …..and continues to haunt as I write this blog….

II

The same place, but now under a new management – more street smart, savvy and swankier the get up and service has become. The hotel front desk receptionist, the one whose tale of woe had brimmed my eyes the last time I was here a few months ago, is not longer in service. I wondered what happened to her and her lot which fate had wedded to desolation and a drunkard of a husband. Standing against odds, this hailing from a rural small town, from a 'backward' caste mooring, had survived in big bad Bangalore – despite being handicapped by a no-good spouse, a marital partner who idled and, sizzled and beat her black and blue ritually for entertainment.

A few enquiries at the refurbished lobby gave me clues as to her whereabouts, and more. The simple earthy girl that had so moved me, wasn't so anymore. She no longer was the silently suffering sari clad woebegone Cinderella. She had arrived, and the city wolves had welcomed her now. She now was, the hushed female voice behind the desk told me, shacked up in a posh apartment with a realtor who paid for her upkeep and captivity. She dressed to kill, drove around in a new Maruti Zen, left a trail of expensive perfume as she sashayed down Commercial Street, busy shopping with her partner, a sugar daddy. Her small daughter she'd packed off to her mother back in the village – she was now footloose and fancy, and swam in moolah.

I listened, open mouthed. Just eight months ago, my heart broke for her and her cup of tragedy – and now I'm hearing this.

What about her sot of a husband?

Oh he's around, only now, he mopes in silence, perpetually in stupor – not cheap arrack dispensed for the indigent in sachets by the government – he's plied with endless supply and stock of imported scotch. He's at peace with the new dispensation. He is too stoned to want to know the how and what of the turn around in his taste and the circumstance that brought it about – or too smart to want to find out. He's content with his quota.

Has Bangalore swallowed up yet another victim? Was the girl I knew a willing accessory to the machinations that move the metro's wheels and deals? Had she got to the tether's end of her struggle? The point of no return, driven to the other side of the divide by a lusting society and a wayward mate?

I shuddered within. What a metamorphosis. In comment terminology, she was now a 'keep' – a commodity that will turned over and tossed around, man to man, for a price? Did she deserve this? Or was she readied for the changeover – readied by a unscrupulous selfish sot or a panting gender. Whatever be the logic, rationale, logic, justification for the transformation – it made me sick inside. Was I too naïve and trusting and empathetic earlier? Was the sob story a sham? Am I a sucker, unable to see through veils? Or is this rags-to-riches story, just another photocopied page of an oft read and heard story.

I didn't want to write this article. I doubt I can effectively convey the storm of conflicting emotions that beset my mind. The sum total of what I want to get across, I hate this world.

27

The girl who was wed to God

She saw her fourteen-year old daughter asleep on the straw mat, all covered up in the Deccan's cold. Beside the slumbering form was a neat pile of brown paper covered exercise books. She'd finished her homework and was now lost in sleep. The mother tiptoed up to the child and gently pulled the blanket over the child's bare face. It was chill. She then picked up books and shelved them. The child wouldn't need these anymore. At crack of dawn, she'd be ritually bathed, bedecked and taken in a procession along the road – and she'd be married off, to the deity at the Yellammadevi. Her only child, was fated to become another like her – yet another devadasi.

The mother wiped a tear that built up in her eye as her mind swam back to fifteen years ago – when she herself had been roused awake one cold morning whilst it was till dark. He mother had pledged her to the service of the Goddess – in return for the birth a son after a procession of daughters. She herself had been the eldest, and was readied like a sacrificial offering. Her ritualistic dips in three sacred ponds, her forehead smeared turmeric and kumkum smeared, her neck bedecked with cowry shells…her head was force flexed low as the priest had tied a yellow cord by proxy. A flower garlanded copper pot was place atop her hair - from now, she would serve – as a divinity ordained temple dancer or in simpler terms, a sanctified 'prostitute'.

The devadasi cult was rife and widely prevalent here, in Saundatti, her home village, and in a few parts of parts of north Karnataka and Andhra. A mythic tale of a sage who doubts his wife's fidelity – of his sons and their role in defying him and of the one among them who obeyed his father to behead his adulterous mother. A then the curse of the wronged woman, for generations thereafter, condemning unfaithful sons to become eunuchs and women to serve her as temple courtesans. Almost every third house in her tiny hamlet had one or more girls dedicated to Yellamma, the all powerful all seeing deity that presided over this swathe of land.

She remembered with a wince of how the man, whose mistress she eventually became had savagely mauled her one dark night as she lay shivering and terrorized in a strange house. Her tiny breast had throbbed as he dug his stubby fingers into them and thrust himself into her like a barbarian. The smell of liquor and sweat. She couldn't even walk for days, and her red welts burnt like fire as she bathed in the stinging cold water of the well. Her urine was bloody and her inner thighs ached and singed. That was along time ago, today, she was a seasoned pro, and knew how to please the man who had become her sponsor and benefactor. He had cared well, and decked her with gold and silk. Although her 'dedication' forbid jewelry, which woman can resist ornamentation, she'd saved them up for a rainy day......

She had seen the world now, the deceit, the abductions, the traffic in women, kidnapping, selling, trading, bartering – of young girls from the drought prone Deccan – the endless migration of merchandize – organized prostitution, to Mumbai. Kolkutta…Bangalore..and even beyond shore. What had the world in store for a devadasi's daughter? She had trembled.

And decided. Better here, serving Yellama. Near here. She was pretty, this teen girl of hers. She was certain someone big, a landed patil or yejamaan would find her so too…Hopefully, he would be kind and generous…like her own paramour had been. Was she doing right? How can anyone question this? I am doing it for our Yellama…what can be wrong about faith in the dispensations of the divine Devi? Far better to circumambulate the temple precincts on a full moon night devotion as her devadasi rituals demanded than gyrate suggestively intoxicated in a red-light bar in Kamathipura…or strip under duress for a third rate video production in Kodambakkam. Thankfully, sleep drowns the mother's anguished reverie. Blissfully too, sleep keeps a little teen girl, unaware of what kismet awaits her from tomorrow….a sentence of a dedicated jogathi, for life

28

The ideal woman

Part I

He was always with the best looking dames in the college. He courted and wooed the prettiest only, and they fell for his charms like ninepins. We, the less gifted, envied – and cussed. He got mail, cards, smelling of anais anais, or bulky envelopes with lipstick marks. And he was forever on the phone, some female or other coochy - cooed with him, all day, all night. Every blessed day of the year. He was a decent chap, with his priorities well slotted. He was good in academics too. A deadly combination of looks and books.

What is your ideal woman? I asked him. Well, she must be smashing good looking, with raven hair, and flawless complexion. She must also be rich, and a sport, and an intelligent companion. She must be well read, and represent everything that's paragon in feminity. That's my ideal woman. Find her, I'll marry her!

Tall order that, I mused. But, if he had his way in life, he would land up with one just like that he desired.

I went my way. He went his. We did meet or write sporadically. Six years after we passed we met up again, some examination work took me for a few days to his city. He was doing okay. He picked me up on a scooter, riding me to his second floor apartment. A sparsely furnished house, no frills, nothing fancy. In a small carton in the porch had two small wriggling puppies. Mongrels. But he looked extremely cheerful. He laughed and cracked jokes. My wife, Shanthi is gone shopping, so we'll wait awhile, she can cook us something, at least she'll give us a good cuppa filter coffee.

We talked about old times, and guffawed loud. A knock on the door interrupted our hilarious conversation. He jumped up from the chair, and fair ran to the door. Hardly opening it, before he yelled out in glee,

"Hey Shanthi, you must meet Kumar. Remember I told you about the fellow who was with me in college, who wore long hair, and closed the college for months…this is that Kumar…and he still has his hair long…ha ha ha!

It was then that I saw Shanti. She was dark, squat, and very plain looking. In fact, she was a let down in eyes. Not for this chap. Not this one, she was so, well, er, ahem, ordinary.

She flashed a toothy smile, and quickly went up to the cardboard box that housed the two puppies I had seen earlier. She patted their backs, and uttered strange doggie sweet nothings to them as they snoozed. Then she said she'd make something for us, and disappeared into the kitchen. In half an hour, she was serving us hot crispy dosas, the kind you get in fancy restaurants. With divine chutney too. I ate four at one go. Then the steaming coffee, boy, nirvana.

She sat herself down on the table with us, and served her husband with reverence, another dosa, maybe half? They laughed and chatted like friends. I noticed she had a discernable squint too when she looked my way and asked, some more coffee?

Two hours later, I was leaving. I thanked her for the nice evening. He said he'd drop me. We climbed down the stairs together. Gosh, I forgot the bike keys, he says, as we turn to go up again. He knocks the door, and she opens it, wide eyed and worried. Anything amiss looks. Just my bike keys, he says, going past her as she stands in the doorway. I notice she has red eyes. Crying? I was sure, she was sobbing. In fact I even saw a small part of a wiped out stream of tear. He was back, and we were off.

Just as he dropped me at my hotel lobby, I asked him. Why, why did he end up marrying her? What about his long held ideal woman. The type he had been so graphic about.

He looked straight at me. Not, not angry, not him. We were too close for misunderstandings. Did you notice that when we returned for the key, she was wiping out tears.

Yes. I did.

Did you know why she was sobbing?

No.

Well, you see, tomorrow a friend of mine is taking away one of the two puppies you saw in the verandah. They are just crossbreds. Worthless, belonging to a street-side mongrel. She was crying because one was going, adopted by a neighbor. She wept because she loved them. She cared. She, who can cry at the thought of being parted with a three week old unwanted street dog, is the ideal female I searched long and hard for, Kumar. She dotes on me, pampers my appetite, wipes my brow, and presses my tired legs. She stays awake when I'm unwell, she cooks for me, aches for me, yes, she is plump, and dark, and cock-eyed, and middle class.

But she can shed real tears for the less privileged, man or dog. Not many women I know can.

In her I found my ideal woman.

Part II

I myself had no clue on how or why this guy with 'looks and books' compromised on his own ideal, till some time later.

A car accident left the family devastated. Not only were the victim, parents absolutely shaken, they additionally had to grieve for the young recently married daughter in law of theirs. Young, and innocent, what happens to her now? The lot of a widow in India is sad, and doubly so, if she belongs to orthodox communities.

They had come to dote on this large hearted girl, she was all they could wish for as a 'daughter'. Yet, with loss of their son, her future and fate seemed determined. Till, in a move that shook the staid society, the parents of the dead boy, talked matters over among themselves and well-wishers first, then they broached the delicate subject with the young 'bangle & bindi-less' girl. Would she marry their second son, and stay back here? With us, forever?

In a few weeks, a simple ceremony saw the new widow turn into a new bride and become wife of the accident victim's younger brother. The groom, despite a few initial hiccups, took the girl as his own. Today, more than three decades after these events, they stay together as a devoted and loving team. They have raised two children, both now strapping young men with professions of their own.

She wasn't 'beautiful' in the definitive sense of that word – but she had a divine aura of an eternal 'sumangali'. And aglow too in the reflected radiance, was my friend.

The father of these fine lads, was the very medical college mate of mine, who had once talked about his concepts of beauty, brains, money and erudition as his ideals for the woman he would marry. The girl he married through circumstance and machinations of kismet, was the young widowed wife of his elder brother. No, he did not marry her out of compassion: and certainly, not out of love. But in her, he found both, in ample measure. If she cared to shed a tear for a stray pup that had to be given away, she said she knew of few, who would stop a scooter to pick up two abandoned mongrel pups and bring them home to be tended.

In these days, when news about bride burning, triple talaaq, and dowry deaths is common place, I felt the need to record the story of the extraordinary courage of the widow, her in laws and my friend, to have stood up together to face life's odds, when the social fabric in small town India was a bit more straight laced, and the mores that society lived by, were a bit more orthodox.

29

Pyar kiya tho darna kya?

She looked like an overgrown school girl, even though she was a medical student. Neatly scrubbed look, hair tightly plaited in two braids that she hung over her shoulders on her front. From Bangalore, a Muslim. She was good in studies for she qualified through the state entrance on a merit seat. Polite, silent and always busy looking. She never walked, she was ever trotting.

He, a six footer, smart dapper and overgrown boy really. From Durban, South Africa. For him, it was love at first sight: for her, it took awhile to discover what really was cause for the spontaneous raging emotional highs and flushes that surged inside of her – now she knew – this is love.

Quiet, and dignified, the 'pairing' was soon spotted hush whispering and giggling – sharing books, and the tell tale charade 'combined studies'. His grades plummeted, but hers she maintained, and like osmosis, her intellect and retention capabilities percolated to him, and in a few months he too fared creditably.

The wooing and courting, the walking hand in hand, the riding pillion, the dinners, the ice –creams - trade mark and brand milestones of romance and its growth anywhere and everywhere. They moved year to year into the final leg of the medical course – then, he drops in home one day and says, sir 'I've married her' – her, she was coy and demure, looking red faced at the floor. 'Bless us, sir'

Now this was disaster in capital letters. Hers was a conservative community with bonding, a middle class upbringing and a rigorously zealous religious background. He was a Hindu, long lost to the traditions of the religion through generations of life in faraway Africa.

Not unexpectedly, hell broke loose. He met me after a month of disappearance and related a tale of harrowing chill. Brow-beaten and pressurized, he had been enjoined through the machinations of a partisan 'judge', drafted into the scheme by the mightily aggrieved father, to agree to a legal annulment of his marriage. 'There was no way for me sir, except to sign the dotted line or I'd was finished otherwise. I am not too familiar with the judicial processes here and I was scared – I still am'.

Incredible or not, I wasn't sure what happened really, but I trusted him to be truthful. He must have been hoodwinked into dissolving the marriage by some glib lawyers. For the remaining part of the medical course, he never saw the girl he 'married' again. Nor did I, for her people who had some clout obviously, got her transferred to Bangalore – and I heard from another student who had her eyes fix-focused to the grapevine and ears glued to the eaves – they'd got her married to pliant groom in a low key nikah.

I lost contact with the boy too, for he left for Durban in a year. Four years later, he sent a long letter to me along with a gift, a book. Inter alia the contents told me, he was well settled now, and married – and yes, he had master-minded and arranged for his former girlfriend to reach Singapore, ostensibly to appear for an exam, and with that the duo had flown back together to west, to Johannesburg. She sends you her regards sir, and wants you to bless us all over again – I smiled to myself, so like the Sir Walter Scott poem we had to memorize at school, 'Lochinvar'

So stately his form, and so lovely her face,
That never a hall such a galliard did grace;
While her mother did fret, and her father did fume,
And the bridegroom stood dangling his bonnet and plume;
And the bride -- maidens whispered 'Twere better by far
To have matched our fair cousin with young Lochinvar'
One touch to her hand and one word in her ear,
When they reached the hall-door, and the charger stood near;
So light to the croupe the fair lady he swung,
So light to the saddle before her he sprung!
'She is won! we are gone, over bank, bush, and scaur;
They'll have fleet steeds that follow,' quoth young Lochinvar
There was mounting 'mong Graemes of the Netherby clan;
Fosters, Fenwicks, and Musgraves, they rode and they ran:
There was racing and chasing on Cannobie Lee,
But the lost bride of Netherby ne'er did they see.
So daring in love and so dauntless in war,
Have ye e'er heard of gallant like young Lochinvar?

How he executed the meticulously planned escapade… I do not know – but as Madhubala croons the immortal ode to love in Mughal e Azam….

pyar kiya tho darna kya
pyar kiya koi chori nahin ki
chup chup ahein bhar na kya.

parda nahin jab koi khuda se
bandon se parda karna kya

On my bookshelf is a very moving, and emotionally stirring saga of one man's stand and fight against all odds. The book is the autobiography of Nelson Mandela, 'A long walk to freedom' – with a handwritten line on the fly page......

.......To sir, for standing by us – and love, Dr A & Dr R.....

30

The sisterhood

A Spartan affair, this union. The groom, seated in front of a smoking fire, bends sideways at anointed time and ties the yellow cord round his bride amidst a low chanting of entreaties to the one above and a shower of turmeric-coated raw rice grains sprinkled by a motley group of curious onlookers. The setting is at the Mariamman Temple, a small granite floored and walled courtyard that is the hamlet's communication node to the divine. The chants continue and something strange follows: the groom, bends again in his squatted position to the other side, and amidst a second shower of rice grains, ties another sanctified yellow cord around the neck of yet another coy bride.

Strange indeed – a double wedding, two women and one man!! This is stuff for the tabloids! Not so, friend, not if you were from here, this tiny chilly dwelling in the nether sholas of the Nilgiris. Not if you've seen a middle-aged widow struggle to bring up two growing daughters – in a village populated by a male majority of drunks, womanizers and no-gooders. Minding her business, staying off street-side tap gossip, avoiding gaze and contact with ogling men, the trio stays low, till time catches up – the girls have to be palmed off. The younger one, eighteen, a sprightly oily- pigtailed cheerful lass who sang Tamil film songs as she gathered firewood, and the other a year older to her, her sister – dealt a cruel blow by deity and disease. Polio had crippled her in early infancy itself, reducing her to crawling on two spindly legs. Unable to work, she stayed home, attending to all domestic chores as the other two women eked out their day, working to earn for their keep and hearth.

Close knit and passionately bonded, the women, were aware what was in store. The younger sister knew, sooner than later she'd find a man – but her sister? She was doomed. That thought hurt, even in their dreams. As expected, one after another suitor, looks away disdainfully from the polio stricken girl, instead, proposing to the other healthier sister. Six men, six rejections. Enough to break the hearts of both the sisters and wrench the sleep from their mother's moist eyes.

Then, the miracle! By a strange quirk of fate – the younger sister lays down a stipulation. The man who next wants her hand, must also agree to marry her sister. If no, then its no from me too. In three months, she finds a man who nods. Yes, he will marry both – and they are. The sisters still stay together, six years after they were wed. They are still inseparable; their mother drops in once awhile to see them. The common husband, surprisingly, takes care of both quite well – for I've seen him physically carry and help his crippled wife, as his other wife giggles as the trio board a bus, off to the city to watch a movie.

Illegal? Immoral? Unjust?

Who cares? Not the villagers, who are proud they endorsed the union. Not the younger sister, who found her own ingenious way to thwart kismet. Rural India, always finds a loophole out of a mess, and how. For us city bred and urbane, all this may appear bizarre – but to an impoverished, proud family of three women, this double wedding is divine intervention and blessing.

Are the sisters happy? I really cannot tell, but I do see them now and then, when I go up the hills for my annual holiday. I can hear the younger one singing loud and cheerfully, as she plucks virgin tea leaves from the low bushes, Rehman's lilting composition from the film, Roja, 'chinna chinna asai'. Beyond the shola crest, tucked in the morning mist and fog, I see smoke rising from the sides of a tile roofed tenement. Here, her sister is she's busy too (and maybe, singing too) stirring the pot for the family's afternoon fare.

In all my years I've never heard or seen a more concrete or pronounced exhibition of family bonding and sibling love than this one.

31

The mysterious she

Dad, I need to ask you something very personal, private and confidential.

Sure, son.

Do you have the time and patience?

What are dads for if they don't have patience or time for their own sons or daughters eh?

Good, now I want you sit and listen – then after I'm finished, you could tell what how or what to do.

Dad felt mighty elated. It filled his inside with pride that his young son, now twenty one, had finally started treating him as a confidant and ally – and secretly, he gloated too that his son had chosen him and not his mum to discuss his 'personal' problems. Mums have this strange way of handling kids, a way that makes them impossible for the kid to talk to anyone else, dads included. Why, she'd even been talked to into permitting this fellow to sport a ear-ring... gawd!!! They are referred to fathers only when it comes to demand for a raise in their allowance or signing on a red ink entry report card.

So, what is the problem son?

Says dad, pulling his chair close to the young man

Well, er, er, ah, ahem, you see dad, of late my heart goes a bit jumpy and wobbly and....

Aha, it also goes thumpthumpthump and does it palpitate uncontrollably?

Yes!

Does it send a shiver down your spine?

Do your senses tingle?

Yes, yes...

Does your breath come in short pangs?

Yes, dad

Do your palms go clammy and wet, and do your knees knock?

Yes indeed dad, that's exactly what is happening

Well, son, congrats!!!!! You are in love – seeing someone secretly eh, you naughty boy?

Oh, dad, yes, yes, yes indeed.

Good! Now tell me more about this secret love affair of yours? Says dad, leaning over.

Well, well...er, ahem......dad, you see, mmm...

The boy squirms in his seat and blushes, beet red.

C'mon, come on, remember we are friends here, just who is this mysterious 'she'?

SHE? Who said she?

32

Turmeric hued girl from Erode

This guy, a regular Romeo, was one of the few who had a four-wheeler during the seventies: that is apart from one or two hi-profile lasses in final year, who snootily chugged by in their Fiats or Heralds (one among who was Gemini Ganesan's daughter, now a leading OBG specialist in Chennai). His, an Ambassador had a radio, stereo and tinted glasses – all very fancy fittings in those ancient days. His chosen mission in life was, in majority view, ferrying ladies who walked to college and back to the hostel.

He picked up a bevy of lasses, pretending to be cruising past them as a coincidence – then, filled his car with skirts and saris, turned up the volume of his taped music (carefully choosing his number, his fav being 'paravaigal, palavidham' an old Sivaji hit), rolled down his tinted windows to make all of us, the also-ran pedestrians, go green with envy. Running overtime with so many sorties, back and forth, this guy turned us a permanent parrot green.

Alas, that is the lot of the have-nots.

The giggling damsels tumbled over each other in their excitement as they clambered in, one or two, listing over the preening Old Spiced driver. I've never seen the cad even slowing down for a classmate (read male) even in pouring rain. By common consensus, we hated him – and unanimously, we hated the coquettish girls more.

One evening we saw him alone with a single passenger, an Erode girl. Hmm, wonder what on, we boys asked, scratching our chins. The en masse ferry service was being controlled eh? Looks like, we nodded. No besotted belle wants to share her front seat with another of her kind. That is a universal dictum. So poor Lothario, much as he loved this Erode ebony, did desperately honk and honk for attention, offering free rides – but her presence, and eagle eyed darts, shooed off any one else from slowing down their gait pace. The usually giggly bunch of gals, actually raised the pace of their strides when they heard the familiar toot.

But once awhile, the lady love took the overnight West Coast express to replenish her stock of perfumes and powder – the powder, here is turmeric. Like most gals from inner Tamilnadu, she wore a permanent yellow complexion – a hue which she replenished and repainted now and then. These were the interludes Lothario bided his time for – back again in public transport business, his car ran extra trips to make up for loss of man-days. All fine, till one buddy (read sneak) of hers, long distance trunk-called Erode to pass on info on nefarious activities being carried out overtly, in open air, in her absence.

In a week, we saw the Ambassador Mark II being driven off from the hostel parking lot and from town by his family driver – and in its place, stood a Lambretta scooter. The cumbersome two-wheeler had pillion space for just one, the permanently perched Miss Turmeric. Boy!!! She had pronto called up the residence of her loverboy, told them about how reckless and negligent their son was driving these days, and got the Ponnayya Gounder see red - and tell me, which Goundan lineage doesn't implicitly trust a true-blue dyed-in-yellow Erode ponnu??

Cuop de grace. In one word, wow.

Needless to add, the green with J boys returned to their normal hues, and the transfer of four-wheels to two, heralded a mass celebration - and a very spirited one through emptying a couple of liters of potent and fiery arrack into the mess Blue Star water-cooler.

33

A quirky love affair

He finally got her alone – phew!! Some ingenuity, effort and time it took him to get her to talk to him alone - without the usual hangers-on. Her sis and his bro. Yet, needed to thank his brother for this. He knew the sisters and had introduced the elder one to him.

'Er.. ahem…..I think I am in love…..with you', he blurted out the words he had stuffed deep in his throat for weeks

'Me? I thought you were courting and loved my sister? You were going steady with her weren't you?'

'Well, er, that's true, but that was sham, phony and fake, all I wanted to get closer to you and I played it up a bit with her just to get nearer to you'

Oops! Mess isn't it? Funny, I was being nice and chummy with you was because I wanted to get closer to your brother….just love the guy……..he's so cool

34

Web of love

Much planning was put in. This internet contact, sounded just right for me. Six months and a flurry of exchanges later – now the crunch time. I had to meet her, Simi, for the first time in person. She was all agog too. She'd flipped for my easy breezy net savvy approach – direct and disarming: May be it time we met – and if things clicked as well as they had till now…… who knows. This Simi was too good to let pass.

So I sit down and crank my courage up. It is scary, this first time 'face to face' stuff. I talk and discuss the pro and cons with all my close pals. Each has a suggestion. Debate, discussion and dissection over, we hatch the plan. I won't go himself to meet her, instead, I'd send Rakesh, my best buddy; a dry run of sorts scout. She wouldn't know, after all she knew me only through the web. After the tryst, Rakesh would report back. If she was as lovable as she seemed to be, I myself would meet up – of course some explanation would be in order, but heck, she'd understand – that's what love is all about. Forgiving and forgetting.

After as series of calls and emails the date and time was fixed. I was nervous. As was poor Rakesh. It was a tough assignment for him. The hours ticked by…..after an eternity he came back, excited and eager - 'Phew, she's some cat man!!!' he exults.

Great news for me!!! Now for the next step. I frenziedly contacted her. 'How about next week, same time, same place?'

This time I'd be better prepared. Good old Rakesh had filled in for me had filed in all the data I needed to hit the gold trail.

In less than a minute Simi got back…. 'Sure, next week, same place, same time' 'But', she added, she had a confession and an apology to make. She had been too nervous and couldn't get around to meeting him, so she'd sent her closest friend, Sheela to stand in for her …… 'I'll explain everything when we really meet up …till then ciao…I love you'

So that's how I was here, attending this wedding. My buddy's marriage. It had taken the groom just three weeks to court, propose and get hitched to this vivacious girl. Coming to think of it, they did make a quite a cute couple, this Rakesh and Sheela.

35

Heart-brake

Today? No Sunil, impossible…I've got to be present at a seminar

Oops! That's too bad, I thought maybe we could bunk afternoon and go to see the latest Amir Khan flick

Too bad Sunil…I just can't make it today. Really, really sorry sweeetie.

Damn….that's a huge disappointment Sheels….I was so looking forward to seeing you and maybe grab a pizza after the show. In fact I have already bunked the afternoon

Sorry sweets, maybe next week

So that's how I landed up going alone. Parking my junk scooter in the lot, I dragged myself into the already darkened theatre. It was then that I saw her. Right there in the row before mine. Cozying up with that 'chocolate' phony and fake, Rakesh. I saw red. I clenched my fists mitigate the raging rage in me. How could she…..the b…

I couldn't sit any longer. I puffed a Charminar before I returned to the basement parking lot. Standing three places beside my jalopy was a glistening steel Delta, all chrome and leather. 175 cc of raw power on two wheels…I paused to have a closer look at the collector piece of machinery. Everyone in college knew it was that soapy sop Rakesh's bike. I sighed and sat on my bike a long, long time weighing the situation and debating all options.

1. I could confront her tomorrow and call her you know what.
2. I could just drop her like a hot potato and move on
3. I could hitch up with another chick just to spite this back stabbing b…
4. I could pretend all this never happened and carry on
5. Or…mmm…or maybe

A few minutes later I kick started my antique and rode home……wondering the why and hows of the double crossing. Two-timer. Jilter.

Back home I couldn't even sleep. The sight of the two giggling and holding hands was haunting, like an evil shadow that stays forever. It was late evening when the mobile sang me awake.

Hey Sunil, did you hear, Sheela met with a serious road accident. She was with Rakesh when he rode past a red traffic signal straight into a bus. I am at the Teresa Hospital right now. Rakesh was brought dead and Sheela, she may not make it through the night by the looks of it.

God! How could this…

I don't know yet, no one knows, but a traffic cop mentioned that the bike ran amok, uncontrolled and unstoppable..

I switched off the mobile. I didn't want any more calls or SMS. A strange feeling of nirvana like trance suffused through me as I reached deep into my Wrangler's hip pocket and extricated a cleanly snipped six inch piece of cable from a Delta 175 cc brake cable.

I smiled smugly, my option No.5….it was all class.

36

King Solomon's court

They were once a contented and happy couple. Bad times had seen them drift – and with a divorce and division of estate and asset, one last problem remained to be addressed: the kid. Now, this kid was special, very special. It was conceived through a surrogate mother. Now the dad wanted it solely for himself. Ditto, says mum: she too wants it exclusively to herself. Not to be left behind, out from the blue lands another party – the surrogate mother. I carried this child. If anyone's it has to be mine.

The family courts to which the odd case has been referred to, meets and defers, decides to differ, demurs to reconvene and adjourns for clarifications.

It was my life source, my spermatozoon that produced the baby, My Lord

Aha! The wife counters, without my ovum where would your sperm be?

Hold it, chimes the surrogate mum, your Sperm or your ovum…but wasn't it my womb? Without nurturing the fertilized egg, seeing it through its embryonic life and fetal growth right through gestation……would the child these parents pine for ever been around today?

The counsels scratched their heads and stroked their chins. The judge knit his eyebrows and furrowed his forehead. The mother, the father, the surrogate and the child, they all claim and rights; Complicated issues, complex case.

After years of dispute and debate, the learned judge delivers his pronouncement. All three will have equal rights: one third rights. You take care of the kid for one year, he says looking at the mother. And you, he points to the father take over in the second year.....and you, the surrogate mother shall keep the child during its third year. The cycle will repeat till the child reaches eighteen, when it will decide what or who it needs or wants. In a trice the lawyers were up......how can this order be implemented? It is already...... the judge shut them up: you had two decades to settle the problem yourselves, now do it our way. He banged the gavel on the polished table to seal the case as closed.

Walking along a corridor on my way out of the final day of the case, I saw leaning against the parapet of the staircase of the court, the youngster who was the bone of contention, the son the three parties had squabbled over. Of course he wasn't a child anymore. I could be wrong, but I am sure I saw the lad smiling to himself: a very wry sardonic one at that. He had turned eighteen yesterday.

37

Puppy love

Less than a year ago, he had stood on the doorstep of this new clinic, staring with trepidation at his own nameplate nailed to the wall. In bright blue, it read 'Dr. Sunil Varma, M.V.Sc. Consultant Veterinarian'. From early boyhood he had always wanted to be a vet and had worked strenuously to become one, specializing in canines. He had pored over job openings and after debate and much daring, decided to venture solo. He assessed locales showing potential for career growth, choosing Ooty, a hill-station in the Nilgiris Blue Mountain ranges of south India; Teeming with retired army officers and tea-planters, every one of them rich enough to afford pedigree dogs and lonely enough to need more than one of them for companionship.

His clientele grew, partly because he happened to be the only Cyanologist around, but also because he was good at work. Soon, his bank-balance had him splurge on a swanky car and rent a quaint 'tucked-in-mists' cottage.One late icy evening, as Dr. Sunil was shutting for the day, he spotted a pretty-as-a-picture young lady, agitatedly rush in.

'Please, please, Dr. Sunil Varma, can you do something for Tarzan?'

Though Sunil was a trim, healthy, handsome, five foot ten macho male with 'lady-killer' looks, he had always held his hormones in rein: His stoic bachelor-hood was dictated, in part, by an upbringing where middle-class morality was integral, and partly, that he wanted building a career as prelude to romance or matrimony – yet, this girl, now in his chamber with a tiny puppy in her hands, churned his insides. A tsunami of hormones had Sunil's cheeks burning, heart palpitating and thighs quivering. Boy! She was class - petite with pageboy do, a bang of locks tumbling over her forehead. The saucer-like eyes, accentuated an impishly innocent paedomorphic persona. Much of what she said, between sobs, Sunil didn't comprehend, wholly due to the proximity of her distracting attractiveness.

But no vet needs preambles; he needs symptoms and signs: It took him two minutes to shake his head. The month old puppy, chocolate brown spaniel, Tarzan, was a mess: it had a sinking heart, dying pulse and bloated belly - volvulus.

A paroxysm of shrill sobs rent the room and cataracts of tears brimmed over her big back eyes. Between sniffs and sighs and shuddering shoulders, she spluttered.

'Boohoo, can't you do anything doc? Please, I love Tarzan'...

He didn't reply. Tarzan's brief existence was over.....the pup lay limp and lifeless.

'There, there, madam', he said, 'wipe yourself', handing her a wad of surgical cotton.

She dabbed her eyes and nose, back turned her to him, embarrassed by the intensity of her emotions. Sunil felt an overpowering urge to hold her close and soothe her searing ache. Ethics, professional ethics...something inside him whispered and he tucked his hands into the safe confines of his white coat's spacious pockets.

'Fees?' she asks, digging into her handbag.

'Nothing.….I never charge for patients I don't serve or save'.

'Thank you Dr. Varma', her voice tinkled as it regained its composure and control. 'I'll miss Tarzan terribly……. I need a favor…if you chance upon a pup as adorable as my Tarzan, puleeeeze promise you'll call me'

She hastily scribbled her cell number on a blank page of his prescription pad, then turned and left, wrapping herself in a shawl, walking off into the chill of night, cradling a lifeless bundle in her arms.

He couldn't sleep: he tossed and turned all night, the hauntingly beautiful face appearing and reappearing in his mind's ken. Was she real? Had he 'fallen in love' with one he had spent less than ten minutes with? Can anyone flip for someone this fast, this totally? Yes, yes …his heart thudded.

Arriving at his clinic the next morning, he was surprised to see someone already waiting. No sooner had he stepped in, when the sixty something army-type personality walked in, sat down ramrod stiff and in a clipped voice addressed Sunil in a no-nonsense way.

'Dr. Varma, first promise you will not say no?'

Sunil hedged, but caller continued, 'You see I have this just-weaned puppy which refuses to eat or suckle. I made an error of judgment, buying it at the Kennel Club show last week: Now, I have a starving pup and as bad luck would have it, I've been ordered to a review meeting of the ordnance committee at our Wellingdon headquarters. A bloody mess!! Snafu - as we army call it. Two full days, out of station'

'So?' Sunil butted, 'where do I come in?'

'Well doctor, I must leave the pup with you. You vet chaps know how to feed it' and then, he added, looking at the open window behind Sunil, 'find it a loving new gentle owner…someone who loves dogs as much we both do'.

Without waiting for him to respond, the visitor clapped his palms to have a uniformed batman trot in with a hamper. Tucked inside was the most lively and lovable mutt Sunil had ever seen: It fair leapt out of its confines as he reached for it and slurped its little red tongue all over his neck and cheek. If ever there was a canid personification of Dennis the menace, it had to be this beady-eyed ball of fur.

'Right doctor', the visitor says, and without as much as a thank you (or sorry) clicks his heels and marches out of his clinic, batman tagging, but not before pronouncing,

'Doc, my bridge partners tell me you are an eligible bachelor with much free time on your hands and much love to share……so you're just the person to care for an orphaned puppy? Maybe you should drop in at one of our regimental ball sometime: you will bump into some gushing mem - sahibs, their nubile daughters in tow, hunting for matches and catches…..hahaha'

Excuse me!! Sunil screamed: but none was around to hear. Bah!! The gall, cheek, sauce and sass of the typically impudent military kind, barking orders before vanishing from the frontlines. Damn! Sunil muttered, banging his fist. The pup, squatting beside his chair, a puddle of mutt juice spreading under it, frenetically stirred its ridiculously tiny tail. Sunil melted: this fellow was adorable. He picked up the shivering animal, feeling a tremor course over its warm fur. Strange world! Just last evening, was a damsel weeping over loss of her pet and today, a dastard, who without the bat of an eyelid, was dying to palm off his. It takes all kinds!

Hey! Hold it!!! That weeping willow! She wanted a pup, didn't she? Sunil heard his heart's whisper: Go for it man…. maybe the loss of one pup and the finding of another, was meant to be. The recent events, so like coincidences, were but games designed by the One above, far above. He took a deep breath, mumbled a prayer and punched the ten digit number he had already memorized and as his adrenaline-suffused arteries frenetically pulsed and pulsated, heard her dulcet voice.

'Hi….Tanya here!'

'Er… uh….um…this is me, Dr. Sunil Varma, the vet……you, yesterday…'

'Yep, that was me alright, doctor, I'm so sorry for my dramatics. I meant to call you yesterday itself, but was a wee worried I'd burst out weeping, all over again. So, Dr. Sunil Varma, what's up?

'Actually Miss Tanya, I've some cheering news. I've got an absolutely lovable pup, a four-week old Cocker Spaniel that someone wants me to give away to any genuine dog lover, so'…..

'A Cocker Spaniel? Four weeks?'

'I know all this sounds contrived, these coincidences'….

'Dr. Varma, I'll be there in ten minutes'

'No, Tanya (note, how he dropped the 'Miss' this time) I must first de-worm, give some shots for distemper and anti-rabies. Everything should be ready by evening'

'Evening? Oh no!! Sunil Varma' (she dropped the 'doc' bit this time) …. 'evening sounds so far away'….

'Aw! Come on, its just a few hours more: I have some grocery shopping and need to be back to cook myself supper, so en-route I'll drop by at your place, if you don't mind, and hand the pup over. Now, your address please? (Sunil prayed she'd understand the what the loaded statement, 'cook myself supper' meant).

'Thank you Sunil (note, she dropped the 'Varma' part this time), you're chuch a chweetie, shopping and cooking too! All by yourself…Phew! Quite a drag eh, this being single?'

'You bet it is!'…

Sunil chuckled internally. The chemistry was working, and catalysts as always, hastened chemical reactions. He scribbled the house address Tanya gave - and started counting time in seconds, to twilight and the tryst.

By seven, Sunil found himself racing in his car: the frisky Cocker Spaniel in a wicker basket beside him. In ten minutes he located her bungalow, the cherry blossom tree she'd described as landmark, was in full bloom and glory as he entered the gate. He stood at the door, gingerly extending his knuckle to knock, when as if in anticipation, it opened. Before him, radiant, coy and smiling was Tanya; Once again, Sunil's knees shivered and throat dried.

'Hi Sunny, come in, come right in!!!' (Sunny?! From Dr. Sunil Varma to plain Sunil Varma to simply Sunil to back-slap friendly Sunny - all in under one day! Cupid was afoot and apace).

'First things first', he said, tremulously holding out the basket for her, 'here, this is yours!'

The pup squirmed out and stretched itself up on tiny quivering hind legs as she knelt down, to lick her face with gusto.

'Cho koochie-koo', what's his name?'

'Tanya, it's a she! We could name her Jane, like in - Me Tarzan, you Jane'!!! (note the 'we' instead of 'you'!)

She smiled impishly, teeth sparkling and dimples deepening.

'Sounds cool - Jane', she responded, pressing the furry bundle to her bosom and planting a peck on its wet pink nose. (Oops! Sunil, keep those knees steady)

Protracted goodbyes over, Sunil rose reluctantly, to leave.

'Hey Su, wait: you must meet papa before you go' (Su? His heart thumped)

'Dad, daaddy...come down, I want you to meet our vet Dr. Sunil Varma'(did she say 'our' vet?), he's gifted me a new pup!

Coming down the stairway, palm extended was a stiff-gaited graying man.

'Hullo doc! Was expecting you earlier...'

Tanya stared mouth agape. Sunil felt faint. He was the very army chap who had given him the pup, Jane. Sunil's knees, this time they didn't quiver, they knocked.

'I knew you'd come...military mind, strategic planning', hahaha' daddy guffawed, tapping his temple and slapping his thigh in mirth.

Over the four-course supper served by the batman who wore a sheepish 'I knew it' grin right through, the Brigadier, between sips of rum-soda and ribald non-vegetarian jokes, chuckled as he recounted with relish, how he had discovered

Tanya though upset, had flipped for the young vet and how he had deviously engineered the abandoned Cocker Spaniel pup episode.

All in all, the ending was worth the drama, they all agreed. Alls fair in love and war, proclaimed the brigadier as he rolled his eyes upwar

'If only Tanya's mother were here,' he sighed, stifling a sob.

The wedding itself was simple, a 'sign-on-the-dotted-line' affair at Registrar of Marriages at Coonoor, but the Regimental Mess reception was something else. Half of the Blue Mountain populace was in attendance. Present too, were mem-sahibs, molars grinding in envy, nubile daughters in tow, still a-hunt for matches and catches!!!

Dr. Sunil Varma has come a long way since that night. Beside him, as he drives, is pretty Mrs. Varma, nee Singh. Tanya Singh. On the rear seat is Jane, chin perched on the car's window, long ears flapping in the wind.

'Sunil?!! What if I told you there is going to an addition to our domestic population eh?

'What the..? Aha! Jane!! You naughty girl', Sunil turned around, patting the pet's head.

'Sooneel' Tanya whispered huskily, leaning over as she moved his palm from Jane's head to hold it against her own belly "Aaaw Sunil....it isn't Jane"……...

38

Eden

Hiss, the evil minded serpent slithered down the tree, and sinuously sneaked up to Eve. 'Psst! how about a bite of the succulent apple hanging yonder?'

Hmm! Looks inviting, she says, and reaches out to the 'forbidden fruit'. She takes a bite, and slurps. It is so sweet and juicy.

'Now come on girl, don't be so insular, do share a bite or two with Adam there.

'Okay. Hiss, I am sure he'll love it'

She walks to Adam, and hands him the fruit, 'Here mate, just a bite, its positively delicious'

Adam reaches for the shining apple, and turns it round in his hand. He takes it to his nose and smells it, and shakes his head.

'Anything wrong?'

'Everything. Everything, about this fruit is'

'But the serpent told me-'

'Balderdash, that's what Hiss always says. How can you even think of eating this stuff'

Eve felt remorseful. How could she have been so dumb? She could have talked to Adam first. That cad Hiss, had so easily smooth talked her into eating, God, how could I have done something this stupid?

'What happens now?' Eve trembled slightly as she asked Adam.

'Oh nothing serious. Maybe a colic or stomach upset. Thank God, you took only one bite didn't you?"

Eve looked at him bewildered, trying to figure out his train of thought.

'Monsanto apple seeds, mono-cultured orchard produce. Fertilizer treated. Genetically engineered. Artificially ripened. Chemically preserved. Robot polished and crated. This stuff sucks. No way am I going to even touch it. I could get contact dermatitis. If you only you had ruminated before you masticated. Anyway, never mind, be careful of what Hiss tells you now on. He is mean.

And so it came about that Eve, after a bout tummy problem, was back to her usual chirpy self. The fig leaf stayed on the fig tree. Eden remained a peaceful paradise on earth, despite the plots and schemes of Hiss, the smooth operator.

The total world population stayed at two. Forever

39

Three words & the telephone

Guahati, Assam 1953 -55

Let me try to remember, well six, maybe less or more. The place was Guahati It was childish, but exhilarating. A long twine, two empty matchbox bases – a viola! A kid's telephone. It was real fun. Sanding twenty yards or so apart, holding the box to the ear or mouth, hullo, hullo – than the excitement of hearing the voice that seemed to come from the sky _ I can hear you, I can hear you! So silly, the whole exercise was really, now looking back: all we had to do was talk loud and maybe hear each other quite well over the twenty yard interval – but somehow, the voice carried along the string to the ear, the low bass 'hullo, how are you?', was stuff that drove us to the acme of thrill.

Cuttack, Orissa 1956 - 1958

The first phone connection for our home! A shining black instrument, which was placed like an heirloom on an a low ornate table over a white lace curtain. This was more than fifty years ago, at Cuttack (1953-4). The front slope of the phone had a plain surface on which stuck was a white slip of paper with the telephone number on it. Our number. To call anyone, one had to pick up the receiver, and wait for a sweet female operator's voice, "Number please?" she would ask. You gave the three digit number you wanted to call, and in a few seconds, you could hear a ringing sound, and then 'hullo'.

Madras 1960

Then at fourteen, the first stirrings of love: and she was still around. The clandestine apartment to apartment phone call. Wait for the elders to leave home, and the thumbs up signal from the third floor window, and quick, quick, run to the phone, a big black pyramid, with a circular dial. Jab you small digit into the apertures, and the impatient for it to roll back to its parent position, try like made to hasten the process by forcing the digit to reel the roll back – hurry, hurry. Trring trring, Hi! hullo – the giggles and jokes, and gossip and guffaws – the sweet nothings, the 'on the air kisses'. Just as footsteps draw near, and just before the doorbell tinkles, disconnected the line, now! now! Phew, close call! That girl in pigtails, Meherunissa drives me nuts.

New Delhi 1961-63

In a few years from then, telephony undergoes a sea change. Newer slicker instruments, with pastel shades – instant intercity direct dialing, STD, ISD – the nation was on the move. This is Sadiq, Meher my mehboob, Meher, can you hear me? Yes! yes!! The time lag in conversation across long distance is hell. Long silences between sentences, each waiting for the other to start or continue to talk, then hearing nothing, both decide to talk, simultaneously. Total chaos. Meher, I love you. Sadiq, I love you two. Meher, I love you three…silly interaction. But lovers are always pardoned for being stupid. I love you, three simple words, yet how much emotion they conveyed

Riyadh, Saudi Arabia 1994

Then bang, boom, it's the cellular mobile. Instant and on the move connectivity. Messages, ring tones, camera phones, talk time. New terminology, blue tooth, pre or post paid - scandals – the nineties and the new millennium! Meher, read this one, Sadiq juggles his thumb on the alphabet buttons of the hi-tech new age mobile he has bought himself in Saudi, where he now working. And he sends over a slew of messages, some ribald, some romantic. He can. He is engaged and nikah was around the corner!

It is five years since Sadiq wed Meher. He still is in Riyadh. She is till in India. Things aren't going too well, matrimony, I mean. Suspicions, Gulf-widow Syndrome, enforced long intervals of separation. All take their toll. Sadiq, they say, is going around with Shameem, an expatriate working as a secretary in Saudi. Things move fast. He has to decide. He does, and how.

He picks up his gizmo which glows in multicolor. He dabs a few buttons, and then a few more. Meher hears her cell throb into life. A SMS in on-line. It is late night. She's been hearing strange stories, about Sadiq, about Saudi, and about one Shameem. She is confused and frightened. Ping ping – she switches on her set, and in the eerie green glow of the mini screen she reads "talaaq, talaaq, talaaq'

Telephony has come a long way. From the sweet voice that asked 'number please' to the midnight SMS that announced in cold electronic digital form, three dreaded words. Three simple words, yet how much they conveyed. Sadiq winks at Shameem sitting on the other side of his cubicle at office. He signals thumbs up. He reaches for his mobile and switches it off. The screen blanks out. Shut off Meher, shed of memories – for good and forever.

From the string connected matchbox phones through which we whispered words of love to satellite assisted mobiles through which we convey words that break hearts, we have come a long way.

40

The secret behind Taj Mahal

In the early morning's golden glow, the edifice looked stunning. Breathtaking. Mind-blowing. A lustrous virginal pearl ensconced in an equally luminous pristine oyster shell.

The emperor gazed, hands clasped behind his back. Man's ultimate masterpiece. Time to come will record this monumental marvel as a 'wonder of the world'. He was sure of that. The aquamarine water that flowed by, in the Jumna, acted as a catalyst, enhancing the effect of the pristine marbles. The Taj Mahal. By twilight, reluctantly, the Shah returned to his palace. Neither he, nor anyone else who had stood before the newly completed architectural magic, could tear himself away from the mesmeric effect the Taj threw. Hypnotic. Spellbinding.

That night, the jahan panna, Shah Jahan looked through the grilled sandstone opening in his bedroom, across the Jumna, the Taj simmered in the gentle moonlight. Shah Jahan, sighed. How much longer? How much more had he to wait before the final slab could be placed, he wondered. He himself would be gone in five or ten years, and Mumtaz? What happens to her then? Who will care for him and her. They would become memories and footnotes in the annals of history books. And the Taj? His labor of love. He shook his head, no I cannot wait. The Taj project must be completed, here and now.

The wait to get the project complete had taken its toll on his psyche and physique. His once jet beard was now streaked with white, and his hairline, hidden below the ornate plumed turban, was receding fast. The Taj had taken him a good two decades to erect, and had depleted a sizable part of his treasury. But it was well worth, this dream mahal.

He slept fitfully. Yet, till the final nail is driven or the final brick is laid, a project, albeit the Taj, was incomplete.

Late night, he woke with a start. God! Why hadn't he thought of this before? So simple. Yet so complete. He sent for his hakeem.

The medicine man, woken him from his stupor, hurried to the royal summons, bowing his head deferentially. The emperor had had discussions with him earlier on this problem. How much of this, how long, the pharmacokinetics of this concoction and the therapeutic or side effects of that decoction. The king didn't say a word, he just nodded his regal head. When a man who presides over the destiny of half of Asia decrees, it is diktat. The hakeem bent low, touching his forehead in supplication. He knew by morning a sac of gold mohars would be at his door.

The unani expert rode his horse to the zenana. The seraglio's ante-chamber housed the King's favorite concubine, his queen, Mumtaaz. She was in labor, with her ninth child. Repeated and frequent pregnancies had devastated her frail frame and health. The hakeem took out his potion and stirred it into the queen's sherbet. This will make you feel better. By dawn she would be dead. The silent and lethal effect of the drug would see to that. He waited till daybreak, sitting beside the queen and when all the writhing ceased: he rode back to the Agra palace and the emperor – before whom he nodded ever so slightly.

By midday, hundreds of royal stooges and henchmen, plus thousands from the awam had filed past the dead queen. Mumtaaz was famed and popular. The king, the public noted, appeared lost and marooned.

The cortege and burial was grand and befitting of the status Mumtaaz held in the royal pecking order. As the bejeweled final slab of white marble slid into place over a ready-made tomb crypt, deep under the bowels of the Taj Mahal – the king threw open the massive gates of the monument to public – finally, The Taj was now ready for public viewing.

Shah Jahan stood afar and watched the mourners file into the Taj, like a long line of ants they came, from all over. The Taj Mahal, the world's most exquisite and expensive gravestone, was now complete. He could now sleep in peace. Secure in the knowledge that in eons to come the world would celebrate his undying love for his queen through this symbol in marble beside the Jumna. The only man who knew of his nefarious scheming was that hakeem. But he wouldn't talk anymore - no sooner had he ridden past the Agra palace gate, he was waylaid by the royal guards and silenced, forever.

For four hundred or more years the legendary love the emperor had for his consort has been subject for verse and art, of ballads and folklore. Millions have gazed at the timeless beauty of the 'teardrop on the face of time', the Taj Mahal. The dark secret behind the celebrated and eternal romance however, lies buried forever safe, deep under the magnificent monument. Buried along with the occupant in the grave-pit.

That night Shah Jahan gazed upon the glistening mausoleum from across the Jumna: he could rest easy from today – his dream and its dedication to love was now over. What use is a khabristan be, albeit the finest in the whole world, without someone interred in it? He turned over, yawned, and wrapped his arm round Khairunnisa, the youngest sister of his now dead queen, the lissome jewel from his zenana.

41

Shame, scandals & the Sharmas

Congrats boss, where's the cigar? We his friends mobbed him, patting his back hard, and some throwing mock punches. Revelry and boisterousness are integral spin-offs for events such as this, becoming a dad for the first time. We wrangled a beer party from him, with pledges extracted for more. Even tightfisted men become sentimental sops when fatherhood beckons. Who would believe this congenital Lothario, who bed hopped all his adult life and notched a string of hits – would today show a tear cascade down his cheek. Family bonding, I guess, make even machos melt. Office gossip was rife with his sexual escapades, in fact one tale told of how he sired one, among the three, in the MDs household.

But today, that very Sharma, the uncrowned Casanova, was a wimp. He just held his dear wife Kiran's hand and shed tears as she held his baby up for him to see.

Piling the eight of us into his car he drove us to the nursing home where 'mother and child' were. We stood sheepishly grinning, nodding our heads, and coochie-cooed to the little red faced papoose wrapped neonate. God, newborn babies hardly look human. They look more like cocoon – encased larva. They have cat like mews, with eyes all screwed up tight. Their little red mouth pouted like a goldfish. In my book all newborns look Churchill – sour expression, surly looks and perennial sneer.

I came home, and at dinner told Su about the new arrival at Sharmas.

How does the baby look?

Oh, he looks like babies look.

You moron, does it look like the father, Sharma?

No, I thought he looked like Winston Churchill.

Thought so: it won't look like Sharma. It cannot

What's that supposed to mean? It cannot? What's odd about looking like Churchill? Most babes do.

Not Churchill, you nincompoop, like Shekar. That's who it looks like, Sonia had just one glance to confirm the resemblance and rang me.

Shekar? Who Chandra Shekar? What's he got to do with Sharma's baby?

Much sir, pretty much. In fact everything: You really are daft Coo. Next you will be saying the stork brought the baby. Everyone in this city knows his affair with Kiran. He is a regular cad, that chap, he even made a pass at Sonia - and even winked at me when you brought him over for lunch last month.

I slept late, tossing and turning, ruminating over the conversation and its import. Well, I guess it takes two to Tango – Sharma and Kiran, in a way, made for each other, they deserved each other, I guess. But Shekar? Who would have thought he was in that mould too? A fling with Kiran, flirting with Sonia – winking at my wife, in my own house, God! Incredible.

At three that night, I hear her walk to the bathroom and retch.

Anything wrong honey?

Koo, I think I am carrying, I've been having....

WHAAT? Expecting? Pregnant?

We talked all night long, about life, our future family, about baby names, savings, responsibilities.

Coo, I wonder who our baby will look like, you or me?

A shiver went down my spine as I replied,

If not like you or me, I pray junior will at least look like Winston Churchill.

42

The molester in the nightbus

He sat down drawing his legs closer for warmth. The chill night air shrilly ventilating through the bus window which would not slide shut completely made him worry. Cold draughts end up giving him sinusitis. He wrapped a shawl over his ears and head. Age was telling on him. He remembered how decades ago he'd just hop into the bus, nary a care, just as it groaned off the stand. Always the last in. And night journeys were fun then. Wayside stopovers for tea, smoke, chats with strangers. Now, sixty four, life had slowed his reflexes and limbs. He just wanted this over, this trip by night bus to Mangalore. Every three or four months he took this route to spend a day or two with his daughter there. Sixteen long years, that was how long ago she'd left him a widower. Coping with life alone, working. No way was he going to impinge on his daughter's life and share her home. She, an independent young lady was settled and trying to make her life worth. Doting husband, two sweet children. Not that she didn't pressurize. But, he still could earn and support himself, though it was lonely. Living with memories of faces and voices in an empty house. But with today's communication systems, he was in touch with them, every day. She was, half her. He saw a part of his wife alive, that was a salve and consolation.

Just as the luxury bus starts to move, he sees her. It jolts him. Like a thunderbolt. God! The woman across his seat on the other side, maybe thirty something. She, in that yellow sari. A dead ringer for his wife. Exact. A carbon, no, a photocopy, no, a clone. Every feature, every strand of hair, the smile, the dimples, the eyes. This was his long dead wife. The sight shook him up. How could anyone look so exactly similar? An overpowering urge takes over. He has to reach out, talk, laugh, so much to tell. His frame quivers. She has her husband (?) beside her and she leans over his shoulder as the bus hurtles on. In the dim blue aisle overhead light, he can see her in profile. His heart thumps wildly. His eyes dim with brine. God, woman, do you know who I am? I was your husband. I had courted and wooed you, and we had eloped to get married. How can you just nod your head in sleep when I have so much to talk about, sixteen years of bottled conversations.

The bus slows down at Saklespur, on the higher reaches of the ghats. Ten minutes the conductor yells. In six years he'd never alighted here. He was so afraid that the bus would leave without him. It was too dark outside and he could lose footing. Tonight, he rose slowly, gripping the railing as he eased himself towards the exit door. He needed a cigarette and hot strong tea. The eerie uncanny experience of seeing one so identical in mould and morph to his own dear dead wife had disconcerted and disturbed. A tea may bring him to senses.

He sipped his tea from the saucer, it trembled spilling a few drops each time he slurped. Like an aspen leaf, he trembled all over. He wended his way back into the bus aisle, slowing down a bit as he passed the apparition, still asleep. Don't even ask why or how, but some primal force overtook his being, and in a second he found his gnarled palm on the woman's cheek. Touch her, his mind had screamed and he'd involuntarily obeyed. The woman woke with a start. Her husband stood up and landed a slap across his cheek. He reeled and fell, breaking his glasses as he slumped.

Bastard, son of a bitch, at your age – she is like a daughter to you. Don't you have women in your life, wife and daughters? In the melee, a few more hard blows rained on him. A few other irate passengers joined in- call the cops; No, no, just shove this lech off the bus. The conductor handed him his tote bag and shawl and ushered him off the vehicle.

He stood shell shocked, under the night sky, under the twinkling stars. Bewildered and confused. Disoriented by the rapid sequence of events. God! What have I done? God! What have you made me do? He wailed loud looking at the sky as he sat down on the low parapet wall embankment of the national highway as it wended the seventeenth hair pin bend of the lofty western ghats

His daughter never knew why he never arrived. She rang him again and again, his mobile was switched off. Unusual. They traced his body, down a precipitous crag four kilometers off Saklespur. Why, she had asked herself. He was so composed and cool. He had no worries. No debts. No commitments. Yet, he'd thrown himself off the cliffs. Had he slipped, tripped or stumbled? Had his bus left without him? Was it a suicide? She didn't know. Anyway, the cops said, he was old, so suicide or accident they said closing the file.

I myself do not know what exactly happened after he was pushed off unceremoniously, with a rain of blows on his back as he was being necked of amid a shower of abuses. I was on that ill fated bus. I had joined in the fracas. At his age, the gall I had mused as I landed one on his shin. Why would perfectly sane man molest a stranger on a night bus was beyond me. Maybe, only the dead man knows. Or God.

43

Darwins Point

Cloud nine. That was what he was on, right now. The holy fire, the seven perambulations, the pipes, drums, incense, smoke, laughter, jewelry, silk – the wedding. Beside him sat the most graceful girl he had set eyes upon.

As he leaned over the top pour ghee into the spluttering embers, parroting the mantras and slokas the tufted priest intoned, his mid was elsewhere. Yes, he had asked for the moon. In today's world of commerce, he and his folks would be fools to be otherwise. Mercenaries, some would say. But the best, his parents had opined, always costs the most. They had extracted a pretty packet from the bride's side. Coming to think of it, he deserved it, he mused. After all, at twenty nine few would have achieved what he had. His pioneering and path-breaking research into the human mind and psychiatry had shaken the world. Every learned medical body conferred honors on him. The Time ran a feature on him, and the BBC interviewed him last week. He was India's toast. He had even heard he was in the running for a Nobel in a few years.

He had spent time and sweat, studying mania and manic depressives. He stayed with psychos and mental patients, under lifetime detention and restraint in asylums.

Some so violent and unpredictable, he had to have armed guards. He had examined, made notes, collected samples – the biochemistry, the physiology, the EEG, REM patterns – and he had stumbled upon the Holy Grail. He had noted that each and every manic depressive with uncontrollable impulse to violence, often leading to wanton gruesome gore and carnage – and slaughter of even loved ones – had a tell tale sign.

The Darwin's Tubercle.

A small protuberance in the curve of the ear flap, pointing downwards. Hardly noticeable. This vestigial anatomical feature is known to anthropologists. It represents man's evolutionary descent from lower mammals. The tubercle, is a hang-over from out past, quite rare, but known. It is like the appendix, atavistic of the pointed ears mammals posses. Notice the tip of the ears in dogs and cats – that pointed tip is shaped off round by evolution – yet occasionally, it may persist as a miniscule knob along the rim of the ear flap's curvature in man.

He had observed that every patient in the padded cell and straight jacket, had the Darwin's Point. His establishment of a absolutely positive link between this consistent feature and the latent genetic expressed and manifested as unprovoked violence, uncontrollable rage and manic mayhem, had made him a latter day Freud or Jung. His research had conclusively proven a physical sign that identified psychosis – and had concluded that in the best interests of society and social order, newborns found with the auricular Darwin's Point, be isolated and institutionalized. They may be seemingly normal now, but sure and certain, in a few decades hence, they would become psychopaths. That polite neighbor of yours, with that overlooked ear feature, will turn out a serial killer. Now, the world could identify and isolate the future Son of Sam, Jack the Ripper or Raman Raghav right at the cradle.

Bang bang the drums reach a frenetic crescendo, a bustle ensues, time for the knot. The blessed yellow cord is draped round the bride, helping gold-bangled hands reach out, raising his bride's jasmine bedecked heavily braid – and help him tie the two ends of the mangalasutra into three knots. Knots that will bond his life with hers. He smiles to himself, rich, beautiful and famous – what more could he want hereon? He leans back and yanks the third and final knot tight.

Then he saw it - on the inner curve of her shell-like, diamond studded ear, the perfect Darwin's Point.

44

Love & marriage or vice versa

Oh, she, she is manipulative. Matlabi. Schemer number one. Secretive and sinister too. Forever scribbling notes in her diary: no wonder she never has or had or will have any boyfriend, bah, who can put up with a wily witch.

To say the least, I was taken aback. After all, an innocent question about her twin sister and this expressive expletive riddled explosive reply. The she here is my steady girlfriend. Slowly over the weeks had come to fall in love with her. Charming, alluring and captivating. Within a few weeks, I had got to know her well enough to know her likes, dislikes, moods and pet peeves – and it was time now to move one step up – get to know more about her family.

Mind you, I am a serious guy and dating and courting to me are serious affairs. If the vibes are right, then there is only one way, forwards. Towards the altar.

In three months I should be in Boston. A good offer from a software firm made me hurry with my plans and future. Pressure from home was onerous. Get married beta, just make sure the girl is good to you, that's all we want. Good family, good character - are our only conditions: you find her and we'll stand by your decision.

So I moved fast – dating sites, reccos from friends, well-wishers. I'd met a score of late, but, this one was different. Fresh, forthright and frisky. She was into computers too, and between us, New England could be the best place to be by fall.

As I said, I was a bit stunned by her characterization of her sister. I didn't give it much thought after a while.

A few days later, I was invited over to her place. Met her parents – nice middle class family. Steeped in tradition. A good dinner. I met with her sister too. The gal was shy and avoided eye contact. Was her sour looks and monosyllable responses part of her deep insecure nature. I didn't know. My girlfriend had fortunately given me the background, so I didn't engage the taciturn one in extended dialogue. Obviously she wasn't too comfortable talking in complete sentences.

I moved to the balcony overlooking the city, all lit up with a million neon signs and streetlights. She and her folks were busy clearing the dining table. I leaned on the parapet, and thought deep. I felt a presence near me. It was my steady's twin.

Oh, hi! Sorry didn't know you were here

Never mind, she says, standing beside me and leaning over the railing.

Lovely isn't it?

Bombay is beautiful by night.

So tell me something about yourself, I hardly know you

Me? I'm a quiet by nature. Happier left alone. Not like Su, so bubbly

You are lucky, she says in a lowered voice. Su is a wonderful girl. She deserves the best in life. Always giving.

Heart of gold really. Never an unkind word – she will make you a wonderful wife, really.

That night I slept fitfully. Su was all hammer and tongs at sister. The other had only the nicest things to say about the Su. My mind was a muddle of contradictory thoughts.

I tossed and turned.

Early next morning I rang up the Su household.

Mr. Sharma?

Just a moment Jay beta, I'll wake up Sumitra – she's still asleep

No, no, Sharma uncle, not Sumitra. I want to talk to Pavitra.

I heard the girls dad yell, Pavi, Pavitra – Jayanth bhaiyya wants to talk to you

Boston is lovely. The maple leaves tumble down in cascades of yellow and orange. Weekend drive on the Appalachian foothills was fun. Boating on Winnepesaugi Lake was an experience. White River rafting was exciting. All doubly so because of the divine company I had. This girl I married, Pavitra.

45

It takes two to tango

They met up in the chat room. Over a few months they'd got to know each other – rather well, you may add. How open, frank and candid people become when hiding under the cloak of anonymity! Every secret, every day – in fact almost right through the day, and night. They were in touch. Cyber highway had brought them close – in spirit. Aerial had connected them. Almost as if fate had destined their meeting, that's how both thought of their growing proximity – and romance.

He, an eligible thirty something, earning well, connected to high profiles – independent, too caught up in building his career graph to make time for flings, flirts or serious relationships – until he met with this girl. Twenty four, sprightly, cheerful and what a communicator – full of zest, zing and zap.

Each respected the other's right to remain net-pals. No phone calls, no pics, no intermediaries – just friends on the internet. At least that's how it was, till recently. Then they got closer, and more intimate. God, was is this love? His tingling anticipation as logged in, typing passwords, the breathlessness, the edginess. Must be love, he sighed. The high they got from frantic exchange of messages and later emails – it had to happen.

Why not meet up?

He was adult enough to know the score. Internet romances are fraught with deceptions and pitfalls. Yet, his nagging attraction to see, feel and be near was too overwhelming.

He waited at the airport, pacing the smooth shining tiled floor restlessly, waiting for the intercity flight to arrive: his stomach rumbled and contracted. His heart thudded.

A lady walks up to him, a simple cotton sari clad middle aged woman, forty at least, if not more? She looks anxious, as if searching for someone. She zeroes in on him as he stands, also scanning the arrivals.

Anchor?

He steps back.

No, no, not Anchor. His mind races to deal with the piquant situation. This wasn't the 'Angel' he knew on the net. Hell, what if she really was. He'd just presumed everything, and how wrong his assumptions were.

He had to extricate himself this self destruct scenario.

No ma'am, Anchor is caught up with a board meeting - he asked for me to pick you up.

She looks tense, as she mops her brow. Who are you? Do you know Anchor?

Sure, I am his son

Son? Yeah, he's my dad?

Dad, how can….her voice trails off. She deserved this, her cover had blown. Her playing a young nubile charmer stood exposed. That cad, Anchor, he wasn't thirty one. He must be fifty five at least to have a son of this age. Her mind is in a muddle. Her rising BP made her dizzy. She composed her nerves. She had to think fast, she had to get out of this self destruct drama she had found herself in.

The youngster picked up her valise. Anyway before driving you to the hotel room dad has booked for you – I just have to confirm this. You are Angel, aren't you?

He, he, Angel? God have mercy!! Angel is my daughter. She sent me to check out this Anchor guy who she finds exciting, at least on the internet…..

You are Angel's mum?

The strapping lad stood still dropping her valise on the floor. He felt hit by a sledge hammer.

It takes two to tango. She smiled to herself. If he was a con, she was one too. A veteran at that.

They just shook hands and parted. She feigned she was unwell. He, he just said, he had to rush back as he'd got a call from home.

She watched the young man, Anchor walk away from her life. And he saw her through the huge glass pane of the airport's arrival lounge. She was busy mopping her brow, and tucking back a strand of grey hair her ear. He was certain she was Angel.

Phew, he mutters as he starts his car, narrow miss this!

She, Angel flew back – back to her cyber-world, someday, she'd find someone surely – no harm trying. Someone, young, rich and handsome – only now on, she'd pick on the less street smart kind: the ones who feel trapped in a no win situation, and maybe volunteer to buy their way out. Pay her a price.

He, Anchor never visited on a chat site again.

46

How the playboy got all
he wanted and more

God was mighty pleased with this American's devotion and piety. Okay says the big Boss, "hum khush huye…your bhakti pleases me….ask for any three boons, and you will get them as my reward". Right away, as if well rehearsed, the bhakta asks the first wish. God, give me the prettiest blue eyed blonde a man could ever want.

Okay, poof, and there she was wrapped round him, the most ravishing female God had ever created. "Your second wish please", God nudges him. Right, here it is, God give me the sexiest brunette ever created. Poof, and there she was, the most sultry sinuously sexy siren man had seen.

Your third please, and this time choose wisely. In my view you've wasted two out of the three boons you could have used better, anyway, the choices are yours, but be wise"

The devotee scratched his chi, boy this was getting tough. I really need another bombshell, a platinum top nymphet pet, but, as God had wisely reminded him- he was a bit worried. After all how long could three women keep you happy?

Okay, he says, I am ready for my third wish

Thought it out well? Don't end up cussing your stupidity later. Make the third wish be of eternal help. You are sane enough to know that adding one more female to the two already swooning over you, may not keep you happy for a lifetime. Okay, what is it you want now?

God give me a platinum blonde...who can make three wishes

Smart aleck, smart fellow this, God muses. He has used his final boon quite cleverly. Okay, poof, and the fellow gets his third companion.

Now the devotee and his three consorts gambol and roll all day long in the hay – and when he gets tired of their faces and frames – he tweaks the platinum blonde, come on sugar – ask for a Naomi Campbell first, Madonna second and for the third, just say you want to present me Sharon Stone - who must be empowered to make another three wishes.

And so the wise bhakta lived happily ever after, in fact he is in his eighties now, still smooching and tweaking nubile flesh. Of course you know him, who doesn't? His name? you guessed right, it is Hugh Hefner

47

A fairy tale from yore

Two women, both claiming to be the only wife – the situation was sticky. With the position was at disposal of the wife was treasury worth millions. The husband, the young zamindar, just twenty six, couldn't cope with this. One was his wife, but the other, despite his vehement denials insisted she too was wife. Though in the days when this story was set, men could and did marry more than once – this man wasn't one of them. He had time, he was still young, and a second or even a third, quite a norm in his gene tree, could wait.

The matters reached such an ugly pass that the matter went right up to the Samrat's Maansingh, the Maharaja's durbar. The benign and wise king had ruled brought smile and prosperity to his people – despite the harsh terrain and scarce rainfall the region was known for, his long sighted plans had kept the court granaries replete.

Standing in his palace hall were the two women, each protesting against the injustice of the other. The diwans and durbaris were perplexed and confused. Each produced enough witnesses and sufficient evidence of their matrimonial status.

The harassed husband also stood in court – unable to comprehend machinations and manipulations of the pretender and –pleading of the innocent.

The wizened maharaja, resplendent in regal regalia, strings of pearls draped down his flowing robes and turban with rubies studded on it, thought long and deep: he twisted his handlebar moustache.

Young man, why don't you accept both as your wives, after all, he says, looking askance at the bevy of belles peering through the stone grill in his harem – I have so many

No maharaj, not for me I am happy

The king sat and pondered deep.

Then, in that case it implies that you are indeed married to these two women already, but are now trying to disown one. I must arrest you and imprison you for disowning your wife / wives, whichever of these that be.

Amid protests and remonstrations, the hapless man was hauled to the dungeons – while two sobbing women wept and begged the raja for mercy and pardon for their 'patidev' – with the parents of the women too joining in the woe chorus and plea.

The raja would have none of it.

Within two months, the king sent word to the two women. Sorry, but your husband has suddenly died today morning. He is no more. I have ordered my palace purohits to conduct the last rites. I now order you, as per the custom and history of our proud race that rituals and traditions that need to be honored – you pre4sent yourself in your bridal finery to the funeral pyre – and enter into eternal glory by becoming a sati devi. The royal chariot will pick you at five this evening.

When the royal chariot arrived at the burning ghats, only one woman dressed in all her wedding finery descended. She bowed to the maharaja and briskly walked towards the pyre which was being lit amidst much chanting. The entire population of the royal city was there, feverishly shouting 'sati matha ki jai'.

Halt, says the king. Come here, he orders the woman in tears. He gestures with his fingers, and from behind the courtiers emerges her husband. Very much alive and all awash with wreaths of smile. While awe fills the assembly, the sage king speaks:

This woman is your loyal and faithful wife. May God bless you both with eons of happiness and a houseful of children. The subjects raised slogans in praise of their king, for he was wise and benevolent.

As for the avaricious pretender claimant, legend has it she was never seen again.

48

A filmy love story

Like many in similar set up, she'd given up. She dare not broach the subject, not at the hour of her impending betrothal to a boy her folks had chosen. In the conservative environ she hailed from, nubile girls just nodded – they never shook their heads – weren't supposed to. But inside of her, her heart thudded in terror. With two younger sisters in her middle class brood, she could not even suggest that she would prefer marrying the guy she was in love with. She died a thousand deaths, avoiding meeting with or communicating to – this boyfriend of hers.

A simpleton who wouldn't or couldn't hurt a fly. How he summoned the nerve to go out with a girl, was the perplexed query his friends asked themselves. Except his widowed mother, he cared for none; Yet she vibed with him. His introversion was what attracted her to him. A stoic, a sane. How could she tell him of what was around, now that circumstances had made her nod. Better, this way, than face him and his pleas, his tears, his heartbreak – hers was too, she had neither the strength or tenacity to break free. Helpless, hopeless. And heartbroken.

The shehnais and drums hit high decibel, laughter, feasts, silks, scents, fire – she found herself sitting on the floor facing the purohit and the fire – fire? More like her pyre. A tear rolled down her cheek. How could she marry just anyone? How could she live with this betrayal she was party to. A coward, who backed off, that was what she was. Squatting beside her was her husband to be. In a few minutes, she would be enslaved, noozed with that yellow cord on the silver platter in front of her.

The time chimes, the drums tattoo the tell-tale arrival of the auspicious hour. The groom is handed the sacred cord and he stoops sideways to hitch it on her neck.

Hold it, someone yells. A fracas has broken out in the assembly, some people have gate-crashed, They raise voice and protest. How can this be the groom? This is a cad, and married twice already. Stop this tamasha or the cops will come. God! What is this? Her mummy wrings her hands – and her father, he is clutching his chest – this is more like in Hindi films "yeh shaadi nahi hoga…."

Who are these people? No one knows. We know this rogue, one interloper says and holding the groom by his hair: a Casanova, a cheat, a con man. The free for all, sees flowers fly and garlands thrown. Within minutes, the hall is like war zone: everyone yelling, everyone gesticulating. Then like a whirlwind blown over, an eerie calm descends. The assembly, the guests, too shell shocked. The groom and his folks have left in a huff. She sits, wide eyed, wondering.

Her mother wails, and appeals aloud, looking heavenwards.

Hey Bhagwan, what pariksha is this? Why have we to undergo this humiliation in public? What happens to my innocent Sumitra now?

She goes down in a swoon, as her father picks up from where she had tapered off –

God, have mercy, why pick on us? Save my respect in this society, at this my age I cannot stand to see my daughter standing at this mantap in front of the fire alone. Are there no good people around? God, please…

The public sobbing and lamentations are heard by all – then one young man steps forward. The world has not ended. If no one is ready to, I am – I will marry this abandoned bride. Right here, right now.

The shehnais pipe again, the drums beat encore: and amidst frantic chants of slokhas, and the merry leap of the sacred fires, he ties the thread and walks round seven times, his new wife in tow. She, she is in a state of trance. Too fast, too unnerving, the sequence of events has been. She had no cause to complain – leading her in the perambulations round the holy flames is her simpleton boyfriend, now husband.

The couple knelt and touched the feet of her parents, 'Beta, you've saved my family honor', says the father, wiping his tears, as she, the bride smothers her smile.

49

The bride from Hanumanthapura

A clutch of hay roofed or tiled house, on either side of a dirty mud track. The time-forgotten village in interior Karnataka. Development is still eons away. No school, no health care center, no nothing. No power. A few hundred, eking their lives out, doing the routine, day in day out. The sub-post office at one end of the one single pathway, is the only representation of any governmental agency in this part of rural India. A part timer doubles as postmaster. He has little work. No one can read or write here, so letters to or from Hanumanthpura are rarities. Six postal saving accounts, each with meager deposits, are all that justifies the post-office's existence. The postmaster is also scribe and mentor. He reads out the day old Kannada newspaper to a few old wizened men under the banyan tree outside the tiny office. His transistor radio is all, besides the newspaper that connects him and his village to the world.

Tomorrow is big in this hamlet. Lathadevi, the first daughter of Padmamma is getting married. Simple affairs really, weddings are. A knot of people, the bride is hitched through the knotting of a single yellow cord around her neck – and in a day she will be off, following on foot, her lord and master to another time forgotten spot fifteen miles away. The divine sanction to the momentous event being a simple vermillion smeared votive stone that stands beneath the massive banyan.

The postmaster is usually the master of all ceremonies. In the land of the blind, the one eyed man is king. He is also a part time arbiter, judge, and mentor to the simple unlettered denizens in the locality. Today, as the noon nears, his heart palpitates. He frets as he waits for the bus at the neighboring village. Duty requires him to collect the canvas bag that is usually thrown overboard form the speeding vehicle. Once in a blue-moon, the bag will contain a few money-orders, court summons or mail. On the last six days, the bag was empty. Latha, the bride's father, is a havaldar - jawan in the Indian army...is now in Kargil. Newspaper and radio report heavy infiltration by Pak regulars disguised as 'mujahideen'. The battle for Tiger Hill, that's where Puttanna is in action. His last letter, which he the postmaster had read out loud to the wrist twisting Padma and her daughters, promised he'd be there on the day of the marriage. Leave is impossible. Those on the frontline live for today and now. Will be in Hanumanthpura, come what may, on the auspicious day.

The postmaster rises from his squatted position as he spots a bowl of dust on the horizon. The bus!! It doesn't even slow down, as it speeds by, a khaki canvas bag is tossed by the conductor through the open door of the hurtling jalopy....

Inside are inland letters. One, he hopes, with news he hopes that will confirm Puttana's home coming. He rummages through the bag and retrieves two pieces of post. One a money-order for eight hundred addressed to Padmamma, and the other a very official looking envelope.

He goes back to under the shade and opens the letter. Impressive looking, embossed and stamped…a crisply typed page unfolds. Lance Naik Havaldar Hanumanthapura Chikkappa Puttannna Swami missing in action. The official letter details the rank and identity of the missing person…. details of pension, PF and other dues disbursal will be settled after confirmation of 'missing in action' despatches.

The postmaster well knows government jargon and double speak. Missing in action is synonymous to presumed killed in action. Dead. Latha's father will not be here tomorrow. In fact he will never set foot in Hanumanthpura again. The postmaster pushed the letter back into the APO franked on 'Government of India Service' unstamped envelope.

Early next morning he bathed and was ready. Under the banyan tree, the ceremony went on. A few anxious glances towards the west, a few tense relatives…a few tears, drums, pipes and two 'under the sky' rows of elders sitting for a one-course lunch. The eight hundred rupees money order helps.

In an hour the village is back to normalcy and quiet. Men are back at the fields, women are back puffing life back to the embers in the kitchen grates. The postmaster plods back to his one chair-one table office. He closes his eyes and reflects. He could see it, as vividly as if it was happening right now. The tiny shredded bits of paper, of the enveloped letter, as they tumbled and scattered in the buffeting gusts of aashaada. Like confetti they ran, the pieces of mail from the Army Postal Office…disappearing into the plains of the Deccan in the afternoon haze.

It's the least he could do…to the memory of the Kargil hero…to get his doting daughter wed. The Indian Postal Service rule book would be thrown at him, he knew that…. but, he thought he saw, a martyred havaldar salute in approval

50

The first love letter

Sixteen and in love!!! What a feeling…as the heart thuds in her presence. Her every move sends you into a tizzy. Her coy smile, divine. Why does the creator sculpt models like this one? To make me loony?

There she is playing with a group of friends, all fourteen and from standard seven. What a silly game this hopscotch is…well, she plays it best. I wish she wins this round. I stand on my first floor terrace and have my gaze fixed.. this pretty girl in long silk skirt which billows like a gossamer bloom as she hops on the squares…watch it miss, ooops, you just missed being fouled out…oof, thank heavens you made it.

How silly of me to get involved this deep – tomorrow I have trigonometry tests: hell with trigonometry and algebra. I could stand here an eternity just to be able to see her and her swishing bobbing ponytail.

Then she looks up: she freezes for a moment and then flashes the most sparkling smile a girl can summon. She knows I have the flutters for her, and I really think she has butterflies in her heart when she looks at me. She whispers something to her mates and she vanishes, running like a frisky calf into her doorway in the narrow alley where we are neighbors. Shy eh? Playing the coy gal eh? Teaser? Hard to get eh? Question rapid fire in my system.

Look, she's back and she's coming close, scampering towards my house, a small ground floor tenement that abuts hers, she stands just below me in the street as I watch her, perplexed and heart pounding. She opens her right palm and shows me a small piece of paper.

She jabs her index finger towards me and lip synchs, 'for you'.

God! A love letter. I couldn't possibly go down and take it from her. My ever alert mum knows everything about juvenile escapades – she's been mother to three daughter's herself – letting them grow under her shadow and thumb, on a light leash (which had a nooze at its distal end)

I shrug my shoulders to let this 'love' of mine know, I couldn't come down to the street. The Berlin wall stood between us….

She makes a face, picks up a pebble from the road, wraps the paper note around it and throws it underarm, all the way up……it clatters on the cemented terrace…my first love letter…

For the next few weeks, I slept with that letter in my pocket, went to school and even the bathroom with that letter….till life took us 'lovers' different directions. Puppy love doesn't last, its memories do.

As I sit on this park bench, I adjust my bifocals and look around me. The teens today have not experienced that fearful thrill romance draws in its wake. That era is dead. Today teen lovers send cryptic SMS messages in code… ugghs…how absolutely horrid. They will never know what it was to get a love note, with a pencil sketch of two hearts pierced by Cupid's arrow...no Berlin wall or LoC can stop telecommunication and electronic 'messenger'ing... the teens have it all easy and wrapped up these days... but can anything match the euphoria of a pebble-wrapped coochi-coo-chit hurled into the skies....uniting a besotted boy standing twenty feet apart and twelve feet up with his apsara...

51

Tell me how much you really love me

Cliched surely – but we all know how much those in love want to be told they are being loved. The 'kaho na pyaar hai' syndrome – baar baar sun'ne ko thayyaar hain…. The ridiculous expressions and lengths to which the partners go to exhibit or express their undying love makes the study of romancers a worthwhile pastime.

Watch her as she stands tall, her boyfriend's lying on the grass chewing a blade of grass, she extends her arms wide and waves it up and down. That means she loves him that much – as wide as the width between the fingernail tips of her right hand to those of her left. Now, it is her turn to put the same query to her lover. She squats on the park bench as he demonstrates the hugeness his of love for her.

Hold it pal, I cannot get the import of his demo: I am on the park bench on the other side, and I cannot hear the dialogue, I can only see what the couple is up to and am deciphering the content of the conversation from the context of the physical expressions.

I observe he is holding the fingertips of both his palms and forming a loop circle with his arms, his elbows sticking out, akimbo. He says something and then, like all teen lovers, they burst into uncontrolled giggles, falling over the grass – hmmm, ROTFL, that's the acronym. Silly. Yet, I am quite perplexed, what was the beau show was about. What was he saying, explaining his action that brought both of them to tears in laughter?

I watch him say bye through some airborne kisses as she sashays off, homeward. He walks past me whistling 'Knock three times on the ceiling if you want me'

Excuse me mister…

I am a familiar figure in the park, so it is easy to start talking. all the regulars know I am a harmless old man, chewing peanuts and replaying past in my mind's eye. I tell him I'd been watching his dalliance with his date quite raptly, and given my talent for lip reading, I was sure what her demo implied, but what the heck was the import of his 'loop' reply to her query on 'kithna pyaar'. He grinned sheepishly.

Well uncle, her wide armed gesture she says was how big her love was, as big as the length between her fingertips….

Ah, deciphered that, but your…

Mine, my forming a circle with my arms meant, my love was eternal, it just went on and on, no terminus, no start no ends. A closed kinematic chain…

Closed what?

Oh, unca, you know that mechanics stuff

Uh uh

Her gesture the wide armed one, was, technically, kinetically, an open chain. Unstable, you know. Mine, the twin-armed circle, two palms and fingertips approximated, is a closed one, a complete, totally stable mechanical chain.

I was all at sea

Aw uncs, its like you driving with one hand on the steering wheel – that's an unstable open kinematic chain – but place both your hands on the wheel, abracadabra – we have a closed and very stable, kinematic chain. As you know that talking on the mobile while driving is a traffic offence – but you didn't know why, that's because a single hand on the wheel isn't as safe, mechanically, as having two on the steering…close the ring, don't leave it open ended……if you want your driving days to or romance, to last….he he

Excuse me baba, all this is nerd stuff, in our days we just said, you're my world, moon, stars and such stuff. We really didn't need linear mathematics, quantum physics or applied biomechanics…. We hummed numbers like 'pyaar kiyya tho darna kya'…or 'zindagi bhar, nahi bhoolenge ye barsaat ki raath' memorized from Binaca Geet Mala or from the million AIR requests from Jhumrithalaia….

Uncle, you're married?

Yeah, son but split now, my wife------

Sorry about that boss, if only you were more into physics and 'mechanical advantage' your chemistry may have formed double bonds, ya know, like benzene bonding!

I shook my head as I walked back home, picking up a small book on "The ABC of Physics" Its never too late to learn., I may yet stumble on sassy young chick with an engineering bent of mind, who may find this graying geeks interesting enough to discuss and discover the laws on magnetic fields and attraction…

52

The smooth operator

What's your guess - around 36? eh?

Yes, I'd guess so, he said, looking the direction where she, his wife was - the object of her attention was a buxom working colleague of his.

Jay and his wife, Su, were at a get together in his company do to where all employees and their spouses had been invited.

Usually, these bi-annual events though meant to foster camaraderie and sense of belonging – ended up as venues for gossip and catty remarks. For non professional home-bound wives, these events were highlights: here they chatted with each other, exchanged juicy bits of scandalous trivia about this one or the other. The rally also was forum where wives assessed the 'threat potential' and 'bearings' of some of the younger lady members who worked with their husbands in the management.

Whad'ya mean, guess so? She's working with you isn't she – don't you people have to know these things?

Which things?

For gawd's sake – I assume service files record the date of birth and ages of all who are employed.

They do

So, is she thirty six or what?

He gulped hard, phew, close shave that was....bless my soul – and he'd presumed the missus was referring to bust dimension, numerically represented physical statistics - 36 – 24 – 36 and such stuff.

Oh that - he said, she is thirty three.

Thirty three? Looks much older – acts younger. Is she married?

Nope

Why?

No idea

Maybe she wants only the Prince of Arcot

Uh uh

Boy, women can be quite meow meow at times.

Back again, her focus was on the 'thirty six pretending to be thirty three' female. She needs to find a better tailor: that spinster has her top popping all over .....36D, nothing less.

This time he knew what the number meant – it was a direct snooty snide reference to the bust size and bra fit. He stayed quiet, for hers was a statement, not a query, so prudence dictates he shut up and stayed so.

Don't you people have a dress code or something for staff?

We do, I cannot wear jeans and the faculty ladies are advised to wear salwar - kameez or saris for work

Saris with blouse, I hope it implies...she snorts, very vixenish

He didn't reply. This was getting a bit too big catty. In his mind, he saw nothing amiss with the blouse of the lady colleague.

'Blouseless sleeves', that's how my friend Nargis from Bombay defines outfits like this one...he he: she stifles a sneer; she was in her elements, this missus of his when it came to scything fellow females. About time, he mused, to hit back, on behalf of the 'mahila samaaj'

For your information that Ms. Sumathi Rau there, was diagnosed having breast cancer and had undergone bilateral radical mastectomy before she was twenty six – and that's probably why she remained unmarried and that possibly why her bust looks so synthetically artificial – because it is.

That shut jabber-jaws for good, at least for the evening. She was sullen and blue. The information he had passed on, had made her introspective – and very guilty. Good. Serves her right for being so meowy.

Jay, it must be terrible, the cancer stuff…

It is

How she must have suffered, the pain, the worries, the agony…I cannot even imagine

Coo, do you know her well? maybe someday we could meet up – I need to learn so much from her

Sorry honey. She's leaving for Chennai next week – voluntary transfer – she's still on chemotherapy, the poor soul and its easier if she's there.

Of course, it would be easier for him too, that he didn't tell his dear wife – Shanti, for that who Sumathi really was – would be shifting to Hyderabad and that he'd worked out a scheme to be with her every month – the office romance thing you know.

Jay, hold it, what about her chemo?

What chemo? You numbskull, Jay smirked to himself– he was lost in his own thoughts….. that sexy Shanti, she's a knocker with thoracic assets a firm thirty six –D, nothing less – ask me, smiled Jay, as he pecked his remorseful, still rueful wife Su goodnight -

53

I wonder why they stopped visiting us

The braggart if ever there was one: full of himself. Hyperbole was his second name. Anything you said or did, he'd already said that, been there. He was a suffocating, self centered, megalomaniacal ego maniac. And his wife, boy they were evenly matched – when he returned from that trip from Coorg, he claimed he had caught a mahseer no less than thirty three pounds six ounces – his wife, butts in, eight ounces dear.

You actually weighed that fellow?

He diplomatically shifts topic, and did you know that we rode an elephant which was at least twelve feet at the shoulders….

Twelve feet nine inches dear, the female chirps.

Boy, this couple could make Harsha Bhogle run for cover. Perfectly matched, you could add. Married a few months ago, they vibed on the same wavelength.

My pet pooch, a Great Dane with sorrowful eyes saunters in with a lazy swing of his tail

Nice dog. Is it an Alsatian?

Nope, a Great Dane

What's so great about him?

No, that's his breed name, Great Dane

Prema, you remember our fellow, boy you should have seen him, people asked me if it was a heifer or what. How old is this mutt?

Two years.

How tall was your dog?

Twenty eight inches sir

And a half, she chimes.

This fellow Dracs, I tell them, is twenty nine inches.

It only took just two flat seconds for the couple to recover –

Oh, our Dino, short for dinosaur, was twenty eight when he was merely four months old

And a half, twenty eight and a half at four days less than four months honey

Gawd!!!!! Please save me from this pair – can't you send them somewhere else, to Texas where they'd feel at home among their kin.

My muttering to the Almighty was perhaps a bit more audible than I imagined, for I felt an elbow dig into my side. It was my wife. Her expression said it all….she was looking at the ceiling, as if to implore Lord Krishna…please, please.

She quickly camouflaged her gesture and engaged the lady loudmouth with some trivia

I leaned over and asked him, with a wicked wink…How the missus doing? Happy with her?

He shifted uncomfortably.

I cupped my fist over my mouth and hoarsely whispered – I've laid four in the office in seven months

His eyes widened and nostrils flared. He sat back ramrod stiff in his sofa and thundered...

Four? Just four?? In seven months...heard that Prema, ha, ha, ha, four!!...Doctor Kumar, I've slept with six women in the last forty two days...

Conversation suddenly froze. Icy chill. Frigid. Not a squeak. All we observed was that brag biting his tongue, and all we heard was that Prema gnashing her molars.

That Padhu and Prema haven't visited us in months now. I wonder why..

54

The anonymous phone call

Part I

How can just a single anonymous phone call cause so much upheaval? It can, people in the know will opine – it depends on the content of the message received: here in this instance, the message was cryptic in form and chaotic in implication.

Is it Mrs. Sundari Rajendran?

Yes?

Please don't ask who is speaking, just listen carefully

A palpable tremor rode up Sundari's spine. Who is this, who do you want, her mind wanted to scream: yet, the icy voice on the line stilled her tongue

Is your baby's name Meenakshi?

Yes

Well, she isn't yours Sundari. Meena was born on 23rd February this year to another woman in the hospital and was swapped for yours, a baby boy you delivered the same day

Sundari felt her mouth go dry and tongue go limp. The female voice continued.

I know that the switch took place, I was there.

Click.

Not a word more, even before Sundari could summon her wits the line went dead.

A rivulet of cold sweat ran down Sundari's face as she mopped her brow. She sank down and sat on the floor. What was happening? She looked across the room. Peacefully asleep was Meena, two months old. The third of her three children. All girls. Much mumbling and muttering accompanied the birth of three daughters in a row. She had prayed long and hard, yet, she had been gifted with another daughter. Her in-laws weren't too happy with the latest arrival. Her husband, had pouted, grimaced and turned his face when told of the gender of his newborn.

Her Gods had let her down, she had sobbed silently as the neonate snuggled up to her breast in the hospital: not a relative greeted her motherhood. Even kith and kin from her own side of the family tree had evaded her since this birth –

An overwhelming emotion surged over her after the call: she walked up to the cradle: could this be true? What if??? She trembled at the very thought. An unexplainable panic seized her as her baby stirred awake and started wailing. For the first time in two months, her maternal instincts deserted her, for one wee moment, she dithered...doubts assailed her senses. Is this baby mine? What about the baby boy?? Where and with who was he?...was he, her son being fed? A sigh, a sob and a saline drop involuntarily built in her: It was hell till evening, the anticipation for her husband and children to return from work and school. The hushed exchange of information, of the call, of the panic, the devastation. She wept bitterly leaning on an un-supporting husband's shoulders as he heard her incredible story and looked askance. She was making this up, he thought. To evoke sympathy, to draw attention, to throw me and my mother off her tracks for begetting a third girl child....she's making up this extraordinary tale to convince me, that ours was a boy.....not this wailing baby girl, here.

Part II

It was a restless night for both. Rajendran sat awake, wondering: Sundari tossed about, scared. No words were spoken. Blissfully aslumber, between them, oblivious to the cruel realities of the world around, was baby, Meena.

In office, Rajendran brooded and replayed the events of last evening: What if all this was true? Why would Sundari take the huge risk of lying? He picked up the phone and dialed.

Good morning, Egmore ESI Hospital, can I help you?

Can I speak to the Chief Medical Officer please?

The line connected, Rajendran cleared his throat and told the lady OBG specialist what he knew. There was a long silence at the other end: then, as expected, the outright denial, the taking umbrage, the hurried disconnection. Rajendran squirmed in his seat, rose, applied for one day leave and went to the hospital. His demeanor and looks were menacing enough for him to be treated with deference: he pored over the hospital admission and discharge records for February. As insisted by the doctors, to his untrained eye, nothing appeared amiss. Yet, some doubtful over-writings, erasure, and re-entries for the last week, especially the 23rd raised some suspicions. Professional deciphering could help.

He rang up a lawyer, his friend Mani and along with him went to the T' Nagar Police Station. The sympathetic station house officer heard them out. In an hour they were back at the hospital; khaki opens doors, and mouths.

Muffled denials, wringing hands. Sullen expressions. The devil may care look on the hospital Director's face was gone now. Yes, there may have been a slight mix up: but that had been sorted out. No, she was sure, the doctor stressed, there was no switching neonates. Well, its not impossible, such things do happen. However on the persistence of the trio, she handed over a photocopy of the records for that day.

Back at the station, poring over the entries with meticulous attention, they now zeroed in on a possible 'suspect'. No, not the one who had arranged the swap, but the one who had 'benefited' by it. After all, in India, a baby son was first choice for many expectant mothers, if not most.

A police jeep drove them back to Rajendran's house, where he picked up Sundari and the still sleeping Meena: the whole lot of them, accompanied by two constables eased into the Saidapet: past by-lanes and rows of tile roofed houses of middle class Chennai.

Much shock and denial, much rage, remonstration and rancor, and many telephone calls, amidst the presence of many relatives and men, the burkha-clad tear-eyed Maimoona brought the baby she had 'delivered' on 23rd February. The two innocents, both paying for greed and misdeeds of adults, were exchanged in presence of the policemen and a witness, a doctor from the ESI, who had been summoned. An amicable end to a chaotic day's work, the sub-inspector smiled: no written complaints, no arrests, no intimidation, no FIRs....tact, diplomacy and common sense had seen a happy ending to a vexed personal with potential to flare up into a communal issue: the hospital records were evidence enough of a careless handling of postpartum events: some one, had goofed – it was pretty clear; good that the involved parties had come to terms and agreed for an off-record compromise. To restore status quo ante, exchange the eight week olds. Case closed.

A beaming Sundari whispered something into her husband's ear, as she held her own new baby to her bosom. Rajendran nodded, and politely asked

I hope you people haven't hurried with the circumcision….we Hindus usually…

Maimoona's husband glared at them as he replied

Circumcision? Why would anyone circumcise a girl?

Altaf, he waited for the hubbub to die down. One by one, commiserating relatives and neighbors left…he was alone, at last with his wife, Maimoona. She too looked bleary eyed and sad.

The rapidly developing incidents of the day told on her frail frame. He lit a cigarette and stood by the window, he inhaled deep and let the out-flowing smoke form ringlets as they puffed off into the courtyard.

Altaf, you are a genius, he muttered to himself.

It was a long story: his years of work as a lowly clerk at the warehouse at Mazgaon Docks…..his struggle in the big bad city, his sweat to work hard, paid, and he soon found himself across the Arabian Sea, in the Gulf. Five years of grind in the desert emirate had seen him save enough to find himself a pretty Hyderabadi girl from a good family.

He had since shifted to Madras harbor, where as a shipping agent, he raked in enough to rent himself a small place – but his house, dream house was getting ready – in two years, he'd move to Gujarat coast – to his own set up, a shipping insurance agency.

But somewhere something troubled him deep. His life in Mumbai was survival. Along the line, with picking up dollars and dinars, he'd picked up a dreaded virus. HIV. the hematological reports had read. Repeat tests had confirmed. Altaf had AIDS. He left Mumbai, moved to Chennai. Now his wife Maimoona was mother to his first child, a daughter. The local ESI Hospital laboratory had called him over and passed in the information, he knew, he so dreaded to hear. His newborn child was also a congenital carrier – she too was infected.

He moved fast, he contacted people he knew in the subterranean level dirty business affairs: yes, it can be done. Babies can be switched. But it was fraught with risk: and cost a pretty penny: offended mothers make deadly adversaries and defend hard. You need insiders, pliable hospital staff. The plan had to be perfect.

Altaf thought deep. No, he decided, he'd plan it his foolproof way. Good, he had one worked out to the last detail months earlier. A foolproof one. Lay his hands on the original hospital registers through a flexible sot, a ward-boy, make a few dubious double entries, scratches, enough scrawls, over-writings, deletions, corrections, erasure…. Enough to raise eyebrows and doubts. Then to lie low. For two months; then he spent two rupees at a STD booth to make a local call.

He asked a girl at the public telephone booth near the harbor to call up a number he gave her. Just read this line out, he said, passing a piece of paper which had a line scrawled on it……and she did, as he stood beside her.

Mrs. Sundari Rajendran?...............that's how that line started.

It worked perfect. No mother can live with a doubt or suspicion. It would eat her up from inside. He knew that couple would search the records, get their antennae up, especially if he threw in a bait – baby boy, he had to enter in the register – that would be the trump card he'd use. They would come searching, grab the baby in a hurry, and go.

Today, his plan had worked to perfection. He and Maimoona were now parents to a healthy bonny cuddly virus free baby. Their own HIV infected child, thanks to some help from a dumb policeman and an alcoholic OT attendant, was now Rajendran's and Sundari's. Yes, they probably would protest, raise din when they found out the 'son' they had plucked back was a 'daughter', but who would care…not the the cop, he'd be smug that he'd restored their legit baby to them. Not relatives, they' would fret, but come around. Not Rajendran, he'd would cuss, his lot, but take the blow….and Sundari, ha ha, Sundari would be left holding a baby, which was doomed and which wasn't hers. The staff at ESI would rip the offending pages off the register, too many glaring errors…bad publicity: they'd destroy the evidence.

The very next day, Maimoona and Altaf and their new baby were flying to Hyderabad enroute to Calcutta. Maimoona, she wouldn't ever wise up to anything, she was dumb anyway, rich and dumb.

The Chennai segment of his plan had ended as he thought it would, touché…..he mumbled to himself as he blew another tandem of rings of blue smoke into the air staring outside the window of the Dolphin Five Star Hotel in Vizag……

55

Why the frog didn't want
to become a prince

'Croak, someone kiss me? I'm Prince under a witch's hex…one kiss, the spell is off…please, anyone? Kiss me and I'll marry and take you back to live rich'.

As the toad sat wailing, he spots the recently-split Princess Di strolling along with Elton John….

'Wow!' Slimy ogles, increasing his dirge decibel (who wouldn't?)

'Tch, tch, poor thing', Diana exclaims. 'John, did you hear this tragic tale?'

Elton, overcome with emotion, kneels down to kiss. Galvanized, the frog jumps off.

No prizes for guessing why the once-lamenting frog suddenly became desperately

frantic and leapt away……..

56

Coffee for the newlywed

You could say being just married is a period of discovery. To interact intimately with your new spouse, learning new words, accents and perspectives from each other – and also stumble upon traits and characteristics alien to the ones you've got used to among your own kith and kin. The sight of woman's clothes drying on the clothes-line, have a female voice humming in the kitchen, so many little things marriage throws up. But for me, the unkindest discovery was this girl I married was a tea drinker. Trivial? You may comment. But for me, born and brought up with liters of steaming pungent coffee as staple liquid diet and water substitute, it was devastating, How could anyone start the day with a cup of tea? Doesn't she have an Iyer gene in her? Is she a mutant – we all know how that supercilious community regards coffee – why they even quench the cradle inhabitant's thirst by thrusting feeding bottles filled with coffee – and I personally have seen how that toothless junior slurps the brew, shaking its little fists demanding 'can I have some more?' a la Oliver Twist.

Coffee making is an inherited art, much like the elaborate geisha tea parties of samurai Nippon. Or the historically famous cup after tiny cup that Pashas and Agas sip along with their hookahs in harems of Istanbul...Closer home, in Mylapore, the ritual is refined and tempered by ethnic refinements. The beans. The frying. The grinding. Then the polished double storeyed stainless steel filter. Now, we know that it is a double container; the one above has perforations at its bottom and a cap that seals it on top. Just shake two teaspoonfuls of the choicest Arabica powder, now shove in the upturned umbrella like contraption with a handle and perforations over the pile of coffee powder, then pour in a tumbler full of boiling water over the arrangement. Seal the cap...and wait. Drop by precious drop, the hot water percolates and drips through into the bottom container. Collect enough decoction – and you have enough ammo now two servings. Add milk, sugar, stir and slurp. Ooooh, this is paradise on earth. Alas, reveries like these continue to haunt my thoughts all day. SOS. Coffee. Coffee...anyone please...

I guess it is kismet. All my bachelor life I've trotted across to the Srilaxmi Vilas Cafe opposite my apartment – for my daily fix and re-fix. Well, as fate would have it, I was condemned to continue the exercise. The sight, smell and serving of chaya – in that cup and saucer may look exciting when advertised on TV spots, but not for me sir: give me a ever-silver tumbler-dabara coffee, double strong and piping hot and watch me melt. But who can make this woman understand. She just giggles coquettishly- oh, I grew up on Bourn Vita...Bourn Vita??? that syrupy chocolaty kid stuff – can one even grow up on that? What next? Horlicks, Ragimalt....what has become of Iyers these days?

Three months into marriage, I threw in the towel. This early morning jog to Laxmi Vilas was telling on my nerves – besides, that nosey parker Sundaram was always there with his Hindu paper, grinning ear to ear – 'enna saar, veetley kaapi illaya??? Pudu pondatti illaya, raathri poora thookam illaaiye pavam avalukku, ha ha' (what, no coffee at home? Aha, a new wife? Sleepless nights eh? Ha ha, oho, these newlyweds) He said the words loud and slapped his thighs hard as he guffawed. I hate that SOB.

If you can't lick 'em join them. So I sauntered into that jazzy provision stores at Luz, and bought a good five kilo sized carton of the best Assam Grey tea. 'Highgrown', it said on the box. 'Choicest Broken Orange Pekoe plucked from the misty foothills of the Himalayas' says the blurb. If its gonna be tea, so be it – a better brand. The best. Darjeeling! No more kaka-kadai syrup for me – the kind I want is the kind the white dorais sipped lazy afternoons in colonial bungalows…with coolies fanning the overhead pankhas in liveried splendor. For good measure I also bought a quartet of the best in bone china, cups and saucers with gold rimming and pastel shades. Now that ensemble and assembly should make the Assam taste even better (that is assuming tea tastes)

What better day than today, Ugadi for a start to a new road to liberation? Maybe wrong word. Not liberation really, but acceptance. Of compromise.

I sneaked in home, to hear the missus humming her favorite Kalyani raagam…in what I felt was more vim and verve than she usually did. I stuffed my purchases behind the sofa and waited, my self humming Mohini…

There she is, all pretty in a new Kanjeevaram, her head fully loaded with yards of tumbling jasmine…and what's that familiar aroma????…No, its not gundu-malligai…

Heavens!!!! It is coffee!!!! The fragrance intoxicates me, it is just like ma made it....She sashays in......with a tray, no cup and saucer sir, no kakakadai diluents sir, it is a sparkling tumbler-dabara of steaming filter decoction coffee....she giggles, coyly "Happy Ugadi darling"

I hugged her tight: the latent Iyer gene, it had to emerge. It has.

Take that you sonovabitch Sundaram, I muttered to myself as I gently leg nudged the parcels I had bought from Luz out of sight under the sofa.

57

Cinderella: what really happened

The Royal Coach stopped outside their house: two liveried cabmen, gingerly tiptoed in. The one behind, delicately holding a soft silk cotton cushion on which like a prized jewel, was a single 'glass footwear'. Now, what is going on here, and who are these royal representatives? Well, as we all know, they are from the palace sent on the bidding of a heartbroken prince…..a prince who at the ball last night had danced all evening with the prettiest lass he ever saw… an angel. But, again as we all know, just as the clock started to chime midnight…she wrenched herself away and ran, ran right out of his sight and the palace and disappeared.

The only evidence of her being there in person, was a single glass slipper she had accidentally tripped on and dislodged. The guards had found it and handed it over to the pining love struck prince.

Go forth and try this glass footwear on every girl in my kingdom, whosoever it fits perfect, must be the mystery girl…for I will not marry none else. Either she, or this kingdom will never see a future queen, sobbed the moping Prince.

So all night and all day, the royal coach went house to house, trying out the fit of the glass slipper. Not this one, no, not this one. The slipper fit nobody. It was so delicate, it must belong to one divinely beautiful.

The ugly step sisters went agog in excitement: they literally stuck their leg out, quick, let me try, it certainly looks like the one I dropped accidentally last night…..says the first one…oops, that's the very one, I lost on the palace staircase says the other, both evil and wicked. From up the narrow winding staircase leading to her room in the attic, Cinderella, the unfortunate orphan, sighs as she watches the sisters try to squeeze their foot into the tiny glass sandal.

Sorry ladies, says the palace agent, shaking his head. This doesn't fit either of you; are there any other lasses here in this house we need to test the fit on?

No, no, snap the sisters in chorus, there is no one else here. Cinderella, sobs silently, wiping her tears on her grimy work apron. The liveried gentlemen gently place the glass jewel back on the cushion and rise - and lo, they spot Cinderella standing at the top landing of the stairs weeping.

Come on here miss, maybe you can try it on too……the Royal decree says every single girl…come down

The sisters look cross and livid. Rage and rant builds up. How can Cinderella, that twerp, even be considered worthy of this royal privilege?

Cinderella tentatively comes down, one step at a time, terror-struck by the very presence of her wicked and mean step-sisters. Then, just as the footman, caries the cushion with the glass slipper towards a demure Cinderella, the elder of the ugly sisters, sticks her leg out…right in front of the gingerly stepping red-coated royal representative.

Ooops, sorry…. she exclaims, malevolently, as the royal agent trips and the slipper falls to the floor, shattering into a hundred shards of glass. Cinderella never got to try the glass slipper, she never became a princess, the kingdom never saw a queen...and the sinister ugly sisters continued to cackle in derisive hoots of laughter all their life, recalling how they schemed to shatter the glass footwear.

And folks that is how the Cinderella story really ended. The ugly sisters went on living their life as spinsters tormenting Cinderella forever more.

What our children read and enjoy is the Grimm brothers make believe version of what Cinderella could have been, not what she really was. Sorry to spoil a fairy tale, but truth must be recorded, as it happened for history should not be tampered with...even for arriving at happy endings.

58

How Ramacharya fell in love and got married

Ramacharya, what an ancient sounding name! Well, let me add, it was apt for him. At forty two he looked antique. Powerful bifocals perched on his nose tip and a splattering of grey already sprinkled his crown. A worn out pair of old leather sandals, a white bush shirt with white pants, and to emphasize heritage and heirloom, he wore a long red thin stripe on his forehead. He rode his outdated bicycle to work, and once he sat on his chair in front of that Remington Rand typewriter, he would stay put for the next seven hours…tap tapping its creaky keys. Even his sparse lunch, he extricated from a yellow satchel, a small flat stainless steel tiffin box. Ramacharya, was here in this government office for God knows from when. Silent, slinky, subservient. He hardly talked to anyone in that place, which, as is common in offices had a complement of idle bored clerks, all pushing voluminous files or stuffing them up in the steel racks that stood lined along the walls.

Everyone had a joke or two about him. Come lunch, the place was awash with derisive hoots of raucous laughter; it was jokes time, and all jokes were on the mouse, Ramacharya.

Yet he went on with his chores, hardly raising his head, or reacting to the leg pulling.

One Saturday as he eased himself on his neat table, he saw stuck on his typewrite a two line typed note. It was from someone who signed as 'S'...he blushed deep, a love letter of sorts. He tore out the page and shred it into pieces. Looking round furtively at others as they watched him close; jokers, scamps, rascals, he muttered to himself.

He didn't sleep well, 'S' was a prim pretty typist in the Records Section, unmarried, thirty maybe, very intimidating and forbidding.....she was an ice berg, and none made jokes on her. She could freeze you with that cold stare. And she too was a loner. Half the frustrated men in that office had the hots for her, and all the women there were envious of her. An amazingly beautiful loner. Of course the wags had a lot of stories they whispered among themselves on her 'past'... Ramacharya couldn't be bothered: for him, Miss Sunita was just another typist, only, she wore a sari.

A week later, there was another two line note. And again. He was getting worked up. He looked up and across the long room....and there she was, in a yellow chiffon salwar kameez, clickety-clacking on her typewriter. Chi, chi, ketta kaalam, bad times, he murmured to himself as he went back to his posture. Hunched over his papers.

She saw red, her faced turned scarlet...how dare she thought as she gnashed her teeth. On her table was a two line note, from R professing eternal love.

And so it went on, for six months, the whole office in conspiracy and concert, laughing hysterically at cha break time.....ha ha, did you see her face when she read today's note? Aaah, you must have seen his yesterday, oh ho ho....

Then Ramacharya stopped coming for work: rumor had it he had TB and was ill. Three weeks more, and Sunita sent in her papers, she resigned. The office pool was quite miffed that their two monumental 'laughing stocks' had disappeared. It was back to routine red tape and file filing.

A month later, they see Ramacharya ride in, not on his archaic cycle, but on a swanky Vespa scooter…and hey, what the hell is this, on his pillion, with her arm round the geek's waist is Sunita. They were beaming as they distributed their wedding card. We're going to the Gulf after our honeymoon, Sunita said coyly. In her handbag, she carried thirty three love notes sent to her as proof of the eternal love Ramacharya had sworn…while he, patted the same number of chits Sunita had sent him….telling him she cared. What else is there for two people who 'professed' such deep love for each other do, than get hitched?

59

Hopelessly in love

A nerd all right, that's what he is. An unkempt genius (now which genius is not!), but for all or despite that, I love the fellow. Ready wit, great conversationalist and master raconteur of anecdotes. Faded frayed jeans and crumpled shirt, matching a sick pair of rubber slippers. My friend cluck clucked – what a *jodi*!! Me, I am a street smart savvy girl doing my finals in business management. And this guy of mine, he was into some post-doctoral stuff on non linear mathematics or something as fuzzy as that.

There he is sprawled on the public park lawn chewing groundnuts - his idea of a date. Bah! No multiplex movie halls no Chinese restaurant diners no strobe lit disco dig – just an hour or so, chewing nuts and grass blades.

Me, I am a romantic, love to be fussed over in candlelight, dote being whispered sweet nothings to…hmmm, but this guy, he can't even pretend being besotted. Laid back and an epitome of nonchalance. I shook out a bright pink rose from my handbag, a long stemmed beauty, 'Here's something I bought for you', I said thrusting the fresh bloom into his clenched palm.

Aha, Rosa chinensis!!! He smiles. I smiled. It takes time, but one can wear down a granite nerd into becoming a romantic through persistence and patience. Then, he plucked one petal after another, chewing the pink flower till all that was left of my gift was one sickly stem. 'Very rich source of Vitamin C' he mutters, matter of factly. Gosh I hate him.

He thrusts his paper cone filled with roasted groundnuts to me. I shook my head. 'No, thank you, peanuts are for chimps' I snorted. He pops another few into his mouth and sputters 'Wrong, monkeys don't eat peanuts, man does. The simians learnt how edible and delicious the stuff was learnt by the species from man'

I stare at him.

He continues, 'Well, peanuts are underground produce, so there is no way a monkey would have known about its existence till man unearthed, cultivated them and chewed them. Monkey see, monkey do' he said – stuffing a few more.

Bah! He knows everything, doesn't he?

I worry. Will he be a responsible husband? A kind companion? A good father? Will his bank balance match his IQ? Such thoughts trouble me, but I go on and on, regardless. We walk along the street, he never holds my hand except when we cross it, when he grips it more because he needs chaperoning, not the camaraderie and closeness contact can engender. He pauses, digs deep into his jean pocket, extricates crumpled hundred buck note and drops it into the outstretched palm of a fingerless leper who is seeking alms.

'Gosh! That's was a cool hundred! Didn't you have any coins or change? Charity too needs control'......

He stays mum. I could give a rupee coin each to a hundred, that won't make any of them any richer or any, stomach full. But when you give a hundred to one, he will stop begging for the day, rush home and make himself a nutritious meal and sleep satiated. One beggar off the street and a happy one at that.

We walked all evening till the rubber strap on left Hawaii slipper snapped. He sat on the pavement ledge and with a outsized safety pin he had cached in his pocket, fixed the breach: Is he normal. Or, am I abnormal?

60

The dentist who loved cricket

This friend of mine Ravi, he's a scream. Fun guy really. Ever since we were little boys we'd been best pals. As the years went by life took us different ways: I became a fairly successful dentist, making my penny yanking recalcitrant teeth, and he, loaded with family responsibilities, dropped out from college to become an insurance agent. Not good, I am afraid, he did little business, and what little he did was because clients felt sympathy seeing his woebegone expression and signed on the line.

One thing we still shared, camaraderie, and cricket. We loved that game. I actually shut down my clinic and he stayed home, just to be able to sit in rapt attention beside his archaic National Echo radio, which between whistles and static screeches, sputtered out running commentary on the test match. Ah, to listen to the Aussie or English commentators as they waxed eloquence on the Sobers square cut was nirvana. Of course, homemade Vizzy, Devraj Puri, Anand Rao and Barry Sarbadhikari chipped in too…with their flowery prose…wherever the match, whoever be the talker and whatever be the station …if it was on radio, we would catch the shortwave and megahertz as they zigzagged past ether over Mylapore.

Ravi, he's married to a dragon, virago and shrew, all combined into one entity. Unfair you might add, but that's the deal that got his sister married off......he marries this lump and her brother marries Ravi's sis. Thus he got yoked in servitude and slavery. Do this. do that. Done with this? Now how about doing that? Nag, nag, nag.....whine, whine, whine.....glad I remained single. But life goes on I guess. He put up with the daily torment and tirade like a stoic. Yet we stayed glued to the radio, coming tempest or tsunami.

Even though by now, long past the heydays of the radio, TVs were already in, we stuck to our three band set...there's nothing to compare to a radio relay...no telecast sir. At least that's how Ravi consoled himself, he really couldn't afford a brand new 24" color TV, the type that 'neighbors envy', because he was perpetually broke. Anyway, as empathy, I said amen to his views and sat with him all through days and nights listening to the staccato sotto voices of Brian Johnston, Richie Benaud et al.

We crouched close now. History sir was being made at Headingly...twenty four runs to avoid follow on, screeeech... hissss.....and Kapil lofts the ball into the stands. A six!!! Eighteen runs to avoid the follow on, and Kapil clouts the next one into the clouds!!!! Six. Twelve runs to avoid the follow on, and Kapil bashes the next delivery into the sky, into the spectators...another six...screeeech hiss, sssss.... goes the National Echo...screech, screech, hold it that's not the static screech, it's a stamping with rage Mrs. Ravi. Screeching.

She stomps into the room and yanks of the socket of the radio from the wall, standing arms akimbo on her ample hips she asks Ravi...did you collect the coffee beans from

TUCS? How many times must I tell you, do you ever do a naya paisa's worth work here, you and that 'pallu pudungi' (tooth pulling) friend of yours….radio, radio radio….with that monologue she goes into a sigh and sob, who cares for me, me I'm just a maid here…while your sister lives like a princess in my house…..boo hoo…and why should you are or that friend pallu doctor of yours care if my tooth is throbbing and my gum is swollen…who am I just a unpaid maid…

Both of us are still crouched low in front of the silent valve, not daring to raise our heads…the blast was too ferocious for us. I was livid, how could this female do this? Just when Kapil….damn!!!!!

I looked at Ravi, he silently tapped his forehead…that meant my fate, en vidhi, mera kismet…he also twisted the tip of his index on his temple…that meant she was a screw loose, a loony and that she had a mental problem…and then he tapped his cheek with a crooked little finger…that meant she had a dental problem too. I passed on a few antibiotics for her along with a pain killer tablet…..and asked her to come over to my clinic tomorrow. All along the way back on my Lambretta scooter, I cussed and swore, muttering oaths and four letter words…

Next morning the lump eased herself into the dental chair and awned her wide mouth wider as I peered into its cavernous depth with a torch beam. Hmm, we had something here. A huge periodontal abscess. A flaming red marble-sized inflamed tissue, just medial to the second molar on the right, stared back. Not for nothing am known as the master in the 'pallu pudungi' business. This was a cinch. I syringed in a cc of local, and deftly prised open the swollen gum, lanced the fellow good...till a cataract of fetid mess exuded. Then I yanked the goddamned molar out without a bead of sweat. I rinsed the area, stemmed the bleeding and ran my scalpel along the periphery of the deflated abscess, loosening out locked pockets of inflamed tissue from deep within the gingivo - lingual groove...watch, watch it, careful mate, careful, easy, I said to myself as my scalpel's sharp edge skirted the Hypoglossal nerve. This, the XII cranial, supplies all muscles of the tongue. Snip the nerve accidentally and the tongue will loll limply to one side.

I packed a few wads of cotton, gave her a few analgesics and antibiotics and packed her off. She lumbered off the chair like a ship holding on to the side of the jaw like Cassius Clay had delivered a kayo punch...ha ha

I dropped in after two days, we had to listen to this one on radio...nothing can match the excitement and imagining that comes with listening to action without being able to see it.

I silently parked the scooter and tiptoed in ...Ravi was all ready and waiting, a flask of hot filter coffee brewed from the choicest Arabica beans.

I walked in raising my eyebrows and tapping my cheek – gesture enquiring on how the missus was. Ravi just gaped his mouth and rolled his finger this way and that...she cannot talk. No voice. No vocalization. Not a word...I thought I discerned a suppressed grin, but I could be wrong.

Me? I was beaming, actually laughing inside me... remember the surgical procedure I described earlier, well about how my scalpel's edge skirted the Hypoglossal, the XII nerve...and how one had to be careful for that fellow supplied all the muscles of the tongue...well – my scalpel hadn't skirted the nerve, it had sliced it. Quite 'accidentally' too. Believe me. On my honor, that's the 'truth'

I poured myself a steel tumbler of decoction brew and lit a Charminar and switched on the 4 valve set: it takes some time to heat, this ancient radio. We sat for the next few hours, clapping, appealing, whistling…Sehwag, Dhoni a whole new breed of blue color clothed players.

Color, oh, I forgot to mention. That bloke Ravi, the insurance agent 'sued' me for medical negligence – and his company through which I'd paid my premiums for cover, paid him a thick roll of notes, on which the Reserve Bank Governor promised the bearer a tidy amount. Well, we laughed all the way to the bank and the electronic gizmo mall – where we bought a 24' color TV. This World Cup we intend to sit up all night, watching the show in full Technicolor, sipping coffee; Silently brewed and served, by you know who…....

The Malpractice Committee of the Dental Council of India could send me a show-cause notice for gross negligence….but both Ravi and I are certain, if the cricket boards got wind of our devotion to the cause of cricket, they may well mail us an MCC tie each….

61

The ebony Pamela Anderson

The weather was sweating hot. Midsummer on the west coast is hell. The dust, the dry air,. The skin burns. We were driving past the arid landscape, whence we came upon a small cluster of thatched roofed tenements. A village. Lazy buffalos and skinny cattle. Emaciated, possessed only for the ability to produce mounds of dung.

"Stop, stop", my friend screamed. Pull over. I quickly eased into a shaded niche below a huge banyan, the omnipresent arboreal representative of every hamlet in Southern India. We got down, stretched our legs, dusting our clothes. I fished out a bottle of mineral water, warm already, and swigged out mouthfuls in a frenzy. "Want some?" I asked my pal. He was looking the other way. I looked past him, and spotted what had caught his fancy. He had a roving eye, this Casanova. Walking with him on Bangalore's Brigade Road was nightmare. He openly and brazenly stared at every skirt and sari. As if he had an x-ray vision and could see through. The dress code in this silicon city being what it is, he didn't need to activate his x-ray apparatus too heavily. The damsels wore slits skirts, and tank tops. Minis and low waist saris. Wow, look at that! God bless me, she is something!! His fingers went into a compulsive reflex flexor twitch every time he spied the 'stacked' kind. He was a bosom pal of mine, but he was a real pal of bosoms. The bigger, the better.

He had a way of chatting up females. His good looks and ready smile, plus spontaneous wit made him a hit at every party or do. He was a total fake though. He acted an ace palmist to size up missies up close. Phony to the core: and how they fell for him. Like nine pins or skittles. I never ceased to be amazed at the repertoire of tricks he had up his sleeve.

Once or twice, I know he had had close scrapes with peeved husbands or jealous boyfriends. But nothing deterred him. He was lothario to the core.

Here in the dust bowl of peninsular coastal highway, the sparse population, and scarcer female numbers had made him uptight and surly.

There yonder, at the low walled village well, was a dark damsel, bending over the abyss, drawing water. In a jiffy our man had sidled up to the well, and pretending he was dying of dehydration, gestured he wanted something to quench his thirst. Some thirst! He had just spurned the water bottle I'd offered him.

Now don't get me wrong. These village teens are quite supersonic. They are more adept at comprehending the codes of birds and bees than many on the Brigade. She chuckled coquettishly, bending over as she poured a trickle of water into the cupped palms of my 'thirsty' friend. He was looking up, straight into her as her pallu slipped down 'accidentally', as she exposed a generous measure of her pectoral assets, which juggled and quivered with a life of their own. A black bra strap slid into view miraculously. This was ethnic Pamela Anderson, in sensuous ebon.

"Super, very good", he said gurgling between words as he swallowed. She smiled, exposing a set of pearly white teeth, he glass nose ring twinkling. Suddenly, my mate felt giddy, at least he said so. The trembling twin orbs of the wench had done him in. "Will you pour some water down my head to cool it down?" And she did, watching the cataract of cool water flow down his hair and shirt, giggling all the while.

Barely seventeen or eighteen, this comely lass had oomph. In oodles. She had this city savvy wolf in her clutches. He was panting already. Of hormonal origin. She hitched up her quilted long skirt as she raised one knee on the well wall to draw another pot of water. A jiggling silver anklet tinkled suggestively. A host of pearly prismatic drops of sweat bedecked her forehead. Standing out on her jet complexion, much like droplets of quicksilver.

"You're feeling the heat too", my friend queried. The double entendre was obvious. To her though, it had no double meaning. Just one.

"Mmmmm", she moaned huskily, "very very hot", shrugging her shoulders backwards, taking in a huge breath, inflating her already bursting thoracic cage. Bending down, she lifted the hem end of her skirt and wipe a rivulet of sweat that trickled down her ample cleavage.

By now a few village urchins had gathered round the well. Not every day does a jean clad urbanite drive into the village. Anon, not comprehending the dumb charades the cooey and coochi-coo the twosome were enacting, the boys found more interest in the insides of the car, and its blaring music system. I lowered the tinted windows to let them see, and hear better, and more importantly to keep their attention diverted from the well side. Well side? I spotted no one there. The comely belle and the ready to come bachelor had disappeared behind some shrubs in the shadows.

In twenty minutes we were back driving, an exhausted, but fully hydrated passenger snored on the back seat, fully stretched. Back in town, he mentioned that he had misplaced his wallet. Of course he couldn't tell me he had been had, and picked clean.

Three weeks he was walked into my office, a labored gait. He winced as I examined him. Tender marble-sized inguinal lymph nodes. STD?

"Nope I don't want to use the phone, who will I call?"

"No you dope, not Subscriber Trunk Dialing STD, the STD of Sexually Transmitted Disease"

He looked dumbstruck.

"Pal, the national highway along the Mangalore Mumbai route is the AIDS-HIV artery of India. The highest number of cases are reported from this ribbon of asphalt"., I said gravely, "Maybe it is best you get yourself tested for HIV too".

He returned after a course of hi dose antibiotics, healed and chastened. Thankfully he was pronounced HIV free. His dallying with the village hooker had given him much room for introspection. He has a healthier attitude to women promenading on Brigade Road. In fact he even said sorry to a lissome lass, when he bumped into her accidentally. He has lost much of his expertise in palmistry too. Only some of his friends are quite taken up with his new found interest in pharmaco-therapeutics and drugs.

"We must drive to Tirupati sometime", he said. We did. All the way back, he sat mum, his tainted windows fully raised, and his pate, fully shaven.

"Boy, am I thirsty", he presently said, "pass me that Bisleri bottle?"

I switched on the music, good old Viswanathan-Ramamurthy should ease the awkwardness. Good old T.M. Soundararajan croons, only the number somehow doesnt seem too appropriate to the circumstances

Thotillukku annai

Kattiluku kanni

Pattiniku theeni,

Kettapimbu nyani.

62

Happy wife, happy life

Men are often put to considerable discomfort. The wife spends a good hour sprucing up. The color of the sari, the painstaking patting down of the pleats. The hair, the flowers, the lipstick, gloss, mascara, rouge…the works. Then the choice of footwear. Now comes the ten million dollar dreaded query?

"Honey! How do I look?"

You look at her. She is looking at herself in the full length mirror, making some final adjustments to the drape of the silk. A tiny tongue tip swipes across her scarlet lips.

"Hey you, I was talking to you…"

"Uh uh"

"I asked, how do I look"

How does one start. Does honest opinion matter or count. Are my views actually being solicited. Or is the question wanting an answer endorsing the ensemble and assembly?

For one, her sari color is too loud. Then it is hitched too high up her ankles. She should have worn her heels before she wore the simmering length of a sari. Her hair is - ughs. The bun is sitting like a nested lump of hair. It doesn't have a luster today. The rose she has tucked atop, is, atrocious. She

201

looks silly. And the footwear. It doesn't match anything she has on. The rouge is too heavy. The mascara sticks out. The eyebrows are too thinned out. The lipstick, is abominable. And oh, she should have just worn that string of pretty pearls, instead of this choker like golden belt around her throat.

This girl has looks. She has class. She just didn't know how to enhance it. Simplicity, added allure to her persona. Mind you, the Grecian females, never more anything more than a few yards of draping dresses-and how classy they appeared, even in stone, centuries later.

And where is the bindi. Not today. It goes well with that scarlet lipstick and maroon sari: she wouldn't know would she? She leans close to the looking glass, and dabs a carefully screened perfume. Awful. It causes me to sneeze. This particular one is a fumigant.

"I am still waiting for your answer, Romeo" She chirrups, looking at her backside in the mirror. She yanks the blouse edge down a bit. She tucks in the bra straps.

"So?"

"Er um....you look wonderful darling...."

I lied, all men do. The evening is still young. The night is long. One little lie could make it heaven for you. Just say the magic words...and no pouts, no tantrums, no frosty glares, no acidic double-edged remarks at the party, no sour expression, no argument.

Back home. Spent, but happy.

"Guess what? Your friend Ramesh said I looked absolutely stunning this evening...and by the way, did you notice the perfectly horrible color she had on. My God, can't he tell her?"

Uh uh…., did he, that nerd? I bet he says that to every woman he meets. And he must have practiced the sentence a million times too. He's probably saying it every evening to his wife before she comes out for a do - dressed, in a hiked –up red sari, with a mismatched lipstick, with loud mascara, hideous heels, chunky choke chains, and crow's nest hair style. Can't blame the cad though. He is being sensible about the whole thing. Just like I am, always. I say the right words, at the right time. In fact I said the very words to his wife at the gathering.

Honesty? What's that?? Liar? Who me???

Just parrot the magical mantra that equals 'open sesame' to eternal matrimonial harmony, "You look wonderful tonight…."

63

Etchings on a tree trunk

I stood in front of the massive trunk. All gnarled and knotted. Twisted and tortured by the elements: seasoned and steeled by wind and sun, into a massive natural edifice of boughs and branches. Simmering canopy of green leaves, the foliage casting an eerie verdant gray shadow on the parched brown earth. I walked round the circumference, and there it was. The 'immortal pledge of eternal love', an insignia. Of two hearts drawn by unsteady immature teenage hands. Suddenly my mind plummets back, back over the decades: right here, I had etched the two hearts, with our initials, with Cupid's arrows piercing both. I could hear our own giggles. Hers, and mine. The effort to carve the bole had taken us a good hour; but, we were young, and in love. And, what better way of commemorating and sanctifying the bonding, than to inscribe it, forever.

I stared at the hearts, now a wee awry, the asymmetrical growth of the tree had distorted the shapes. Even the arrow was a bit askew. And the etching was a wee bit higher than my own height now. The tree was younger then, as we were, and shorter too, as I was.

I looked around, I was alone. Mid-afternoon isn't too pleasant a time to be walking in parks: I stood close to the trunk, and reached out to the symbol. I ran my, now gnarled and arthritic fingers, over the outline. The furrows were still deep enough to last another few decades. The initials, our initials, S and K, still decipherable. I closed my eyes.

How time changes life, and love

What had happened? Why is it that it didn't last? The total union of minds that was so evident and complete when we were teens, how could it dissipate. Newer roads, broader avenues, more resilient trees? I don't know: but we moved on, with more miles, and fewer letters between us. I still have some of those missives. "I got my geography marks today. Only six out of ten". Such are the contents of love letters when one is young. "Could you please send me a hand drawn map of India, showing the spots where Panipat, Seringapattam, Plassey, and Chandernagore are marked? And Calicut too, please? I love you, forevermore - S"

Childish letters, wrong syntax, bad grammar, yet so full of life and lust for living.

Today, as I sit, crouched by age, in front of an electronic keyboard, and the cold white glare of the computer screen. The alphabets transferring themselves from fingertips into fonts in neat geometric rows, I find it hard to focus, a characters appear a bit hazy and blurred. I remove my bifocals, maybe dusted over and misted: I use my shirt-sleeve to wipe the lens clean, and wear them on again. The blurred images persist. I once again take off my spectacles and look at the crystal clear lenses. With a jolt that jars, I realize, the cause of the fogginess is not external, but from inside of me. A veneer and film of lacrimal output has spread over the eyes. Tears. Yes, tears. Involuntary secretions from the eye, clouding vision, and memory.

If only I could relive those halcyon days again. The tears would have been those produced by euphoria and elation. But today, the tears are of pain, anguish and heartbreak. The image of two young kids, squatting at the base of a tree, inscribing their emotions, for eternity to witness, is as permanently etched in my mind's eye, as is the symbol carved on the trees gnarled bark.

Pardon me friends, I cannot continue typing, the screen is a simmering lake of mirage, like a mirage, of wavy lines and ripples

64

Girls! Bah!! They Always Get What They Want!

Girlfriends forever take mighty big pride in getting their lover-boys to do their bidding. It is almost ritual, this 'if you really love me you'd do it for me' mantra. The hapless boy, desperate to please and hang on, invariably obliges.

Gosh! That mush of yours looks like a toothbrush…it is absolutely horrid, she exclaims, suddenly discovering the fellow she was going out with for months actually had that moustache all along. Yet, this is 'litmus test' time – sooner or later, one half of a romantic pair (you now which half) has to go through this agnipariksha to prove bonafide.

The guy scratches his head. He is rather fond of his hirsute facial possession. Its been his, like a brand identity and trademark with him ever since he was eighteen…yet, now, this new comment (or commandment) had him edgy.

Really? My pals tell me it makes me look like Omar Shariff

Omar Sharrif? God, your friends are daft or what? It looks a cross between a caterpillar and a watchstrap velcro… Now Sunny, don't get me wrong, 'if you really love me you'd do it for me' she whispers huskily into his ear.

Do what doll?

Shave that fungus off

Shave my mush off? Now you are daft or something. How can ....

She didn't care: she turns her face away and stares into cosmos. A pout is forming rapidly on her pretty face.

Okay, honey...tomorrow, says the desperate knight

Oh Sunny, I knew you'd do it for me

Sugar, can I ask you to do something for me?

Sure my Sunny boy, anything.

He mind races – seize the chance. She's all cooi-cooey now and vulnerable.

Smitha, you know how that long hair of yours get into my face when we go biking, you know it covers half your pretty face, you know how its splits ends...and you know how I dote the Mia Farrow look....page-boy cut with bangs on your pretty forehead. Now, if you really loved me... could you lop off that black cataract of yours...that is if you really loved me?!

She spins around to face him.

Sunny my man, I would even shave it all off if you want me to darling.

Gosh, that was unexpected. A lateral kick. She loved her long tresses, like a Kalinga naag it tumbled down sinuously in a braid, or like a cloud of monsoon it billowed seductively about her shoulders. She was ready to forego that? For him? He really loved that halo like comet-tail down her back like a torrent.

He had thrown the gauntlet, and he had lost. Now his mush had to go.

That night, he closed his eyes as he ran the razor across his upper lip. In two smooth swishes it was gone. He hated his new naked look. He even saw a small glint, a tear. He felt his face. God, it felt eerie and alien.

As he lay on his bed, he heard the mobile tinkle.

Hi, its me!

It was Chummy, Smit's younger sister.

Hey, know what Sunny, Smit's has got her hair chopped off….she looks so different. She's been wanting to lop it off since the last six months, but mum said an emphatic no. She even locked herself in her room last week, crying to be permitted to cut it off…today she told mum, since you had wanted it out, so she had to do it, she had no choice….how could you Sunny? Did you really tell her that? Tell he to cut her hair off…I hate you…

Sunny's head reeled. He had lost the battle and the war. He'd had lost what he wanted, and she had got what she wanted.

Bah!!! I hate girls, Sunny screamed out loud as he buried his baby-smooth face into is pillow and sobbed

65

The Mother-To-Be of a 'Fatherless' Baby

The father comes with his fifteen year old daughter from a small town in interior Karnataka. I instantly loathe him. A selfish man, I muse. In a hurry to get married to a second woman, he now finds his daughter is a liability. An albatross. His new bride wants him to shake of this genetic tag: he is desperate, and I see the small built short girl, looking on perplexed as her father negotiates to shake her off. I feel acutely sorry for child. He pockets Rs.3000 and disappears, promising to return in three months to collect her back.

The girl is cheerful, always trotting, playing with the dogs, running to a fro assisting and chatting with Lakshmi, the older girl in my house. In three weeks, I've bought her new clothes and she looks healthier, her hair oiled and plaited, her teeth sparkling and eyes twinkling. She laughs as she squats on the floor watching the antics of Scooby Doo. Then one day, not soon after, I confront her – did you use the phone? I note eighty calls have been made in a twenty four hour period. She says yes, and, I don't want to stay here anymore. This was unexpected. Her father who said he'd contact me in a week, didn't – he hadn't even left a number or address. I for one, do not want to retain anyone against their will. Lakshmi tries to talk to her, some sensible advice – but the girl who till yesterday appeared so happy, weeps, no I want to go. Why? Lakshmi pleads. She stays mum.

Where? Send her back to what? A father who doesn't want her, a step mother who wishes her dead? I am told that she has a grandmother in Bhadravathi – so I arrange for her to be taken back and dropped there. The drama takes place during the last days of 2004, two and half years ago.

Yesterday night I returned from my Bangalore assignment. On the line is a wailing girl. Ayya, it is Nirmala. Help me. The phone is taken over by another sobbing voice, her father's. Ayya, please, do something. Nirmala has come back from God knows where, and she is in eighth month of pregnancy. Some boy in Mandya has messed her life, and now I have to cope with this calamity. The neighbors met yesterday and soundly thrashed the girl, I myself have beaten her – but the damage is done ayya......please. His own story, he tells me, between sighs and sobs, he has been ditched by the woman he married – she has conned him of everything and he is now penniless himself – and now, this daughter of mine is back with an illegitimate baby growing in her womb. What do I do ayya? His voice trails off...and I hear nothing except suppressed wails.

What do you want from me?

Just enough to go with Nirmala to Mandya and beg the boy who did this, to marry her ayya. I should have listened to you ayya, maybe you would have looked after her and even helped find a good boy for her...now, now...I just need the bus fare

This morning I mailed him a thousand: try your luck. As far as I know, it is a futile mission. The girl is done for. At seventeen and a half, the little cheerful girl I once saw playing and giggling with my dogs, and loved gulab jamoon - is a mother to be, alone, frightened and beaten black and blue by anyone and everyone in the backward scheduled caste bylane slum.......

It is ten in the morning as I write this. What the future holds for Nirmala I shudder to think. Promiscuous, yes, stupid surely – yet what a price to pay. What happens to the baby? What of her life? Too many vexing open ended questions. I have no answers for any now.

66

The Five Star Mess

Becoming the hostel mess secretary sure had its fringe benefits. The once-a-month elections to the post threw up motley characters. Some shady, some sincere. Ones who wanted the mess fare to taste better, others to bring the mess bills down, and yet more who wanted the prize benefits that went along with the position – free samples of ice creams, soft drinks and cream puffs (that's to pick the best for you nitwits, they defended). Providing the best menu was low priority: the royal treatment local dealers, restaurants and suppliers, kept the secretary plied with the choicest assortment of goodies for free.

The hostel catering bills were enormous, and the dealers vied with each other to hold the contracts. Why just the 'daily bread' supplier, could, in a year, become the city's premiere 'loaf'er. Free pats of butter, free chunks of cheese, and free mounds of fudges fattened the secretaries by a few kgs each month. Of course some enterprising ones also fattened their purses simultaneously.

Aha, the loaf of bread you are supplying weighs ten grams less than the approved

Right away sir, the baker would come scampering. A quick powwow, and presto, the loaf would weigh twenty grams less from the next day, never mind or ask why or how - the secretary takes his slice of the stuff too. Commissions, cuts and concessions: the secretary was supreme. The month end dinner was his finale. Feasts and spreads, with Gold Flake King sized, on the house for postprandial unwinding. Little wonder why many of us, stayed much longer in the college than academia warranted.

The cozy arrangement went on for years, all hunky dory, till that Jug, the Singh took over. He was born to the job, this Jugs. The five star chef could tear his hair out at the fare Jugs dished out for us. Breakfast, lunch, tea or dinner – the menu was an epicurean's fantasy. In seven days, he had a stereo fitted to his room, in a fortnight he bought a Royal Enfield Bullet 350 cc macho-motorbike. By the third week he had the mess running 24 hours a day: Jugs, was a juggernaut. For the month end dinner, we had Triple Five, and he filled the hostel cooler with beer. Boy, this was a man, whence come another?

Then it hit us. The tsunami. The month's bill was a staggering eight thousand bucks. All hell broke loose. Jugs, the Singh was not around. He was staying with his sister, who had come visiting they said. The student leaders and administrators sat to sort the 'mess'. The upshot of the parleys? One, the bill would be collected in small installments, and two, Jugs would be brought to book. Investigation soon found Jugs was holed up in a rented apartment, with his sister, no not the bahen sister, but a nursing sister. His pad was stacked with goodies.

The hostelites, however, stood united against any punitive action against the cad. They forgave him his trespasses. They however auctioned off his fridge, stereo,

TV and the bangles and gold chain he had wooed and coochy-cooed his live-in girlfriend with – no, not my bike, he yells and sobs – the Jug. OK, OK, say the hostel mates, on condition you pillion drop every hostel fellow, at any time you are asked, to where ever you are asked to, at whatever time, forever more. Amen, says, Jugs the Singh. And he faithfully ferried us for two years on his bullet.

The college big wigs though, extracted their pound of flesh: they recovered all dues through Jugs stipend during his 12 month internship. They didn't complain to the cops about the fraud and defalcation: 'he's just a boy, misguided', the Principal opines, closing the case.

I suspect though, it was closed mainly because, Jug's pappaji was a DIG in the Punjab Police, and a Gill clone it was rumored. And the whole world knows that no one tangles with a blue blooded sardar through his 'pyara puttar'

The powers of the mess secretary were drastically pruned, as was the menu. It was leather poori and dal for the next six months. Jug, the Singh went on his way after MBBS, and we went ours. But we recall, with some nostalgia, the days that were.

67

The Queen, Drones
& Worker Bees

Marriage has ruined my figure

Mine too

Whad'ya mean, mine too, how could marriage have messed YOUR figure?

Yeah, the figures in my bank

Is that all my putting on weight means to you – just a joke and irrelevant similes? You weren't like this

Neither was the expense, it has rocketed of late

Inflation

Sure, that's the problem inflation, not the economic one, but inflation in your dimensions – an inflation that is inversely proportional to my income.

Oh, now it is I who is wasting, is it? Just because I bought myself an exer-cycle, the home budget has gone kaput eh? Maybe if you could quit puffing nicotine we'll all be better off.

Now, now, Mrs. Kumar, don't you tell me about smoking. Nobody dares.

In recent weeks the dialogues in the domestic front had become woefully repetitive and predictable. Sniping, ripostes, barbs, innuendos, double entendres, you name it,

I'd heard it all. All because she'd put on a few extra layers of adipose, and developed the first physically identifiable sign of that deposition in the form of a spare tire girdling her waist – now, we all know that weight and redistribution patterns of fat in the female are chronologically related. The woman's hormonal and lipid profile is different to that in the male. She will put on extra kilos, and those extra ones, will seek anatomical areas like bottoms and waists. That's physiology. But, talk about physiology to a woman who can stab with her looks, she will also bring in the chemistry in her makeup. – chemical composition of trinitrotoluene.

No point arguing. Nothing served by logic. No reasoning. No rationalization. What does a man do about these commonplace and everyday situations? Shutting up is one option. Sympathizing is another, but fraught with peril. Empathizing with her obesity, by patting your own protuberant beer belly is another – that often works. It makes her less self conscious – but again, as I'd written about it in an earlier, such commiserating gestures could get you sucked into a one way street ending in a cul de sac - where you'll find yourself pumping iron, jumping like a jackass to aerobic music, or trotting like a mule along the city streets as a jogger. I ruminated over all the choices and options, rejecting them one by one. Impractical. Impossible. Irritating. Idiotic. Insane

I waited for her to switch off the lights, after she was through weighing herself on the bedside scales thrice. I eased my arm over her supine form.

Su, you know something, in a way I am happy you are five kilos more than you were – I loved you so much when you were 52 Ks, my queen bee, and now I love you more, now that I have 5000 extra grams of Su to love – what more does a man want? A little more love, and a little more to love.

I saw her heave and roll over, boy she was a regular barrel these days

Koo, you're so sweet. What a nice way to say you love me. I love you my king bee.

Su, there are no king honey bees. A hive has only a Maharani B, drones and workers.

Oh! Okay then, thanks my super-duper drone bee

Not a drone. That fellow he just messes around with the queen and has day long siestas – me, just an anonymous worker bee, slogging all day to feed the corpulent Queen B and nurtures her brood with honey.

That's sad isn't it Coo?

What is?

The worker-bees lot. Struggling all day to inflate the queen and stuff honey into her mouth. Coo, how come you know so much about bees?

Oh, Su, for heaven's sake, I am a worker bee, I should know my lineage and lore.

And the empress, she does nothing except eat, sleep, procreate and amuse herself with the drones?

Yup.

Serves her right. No wonder she is obese.

Indeed my Maharani, indeed. No wonder at all. I saw her roll back. Sorry, not saw, but felt. Her girth and waist and bottom circumference

68

Sex, Gore & Hostels: The Ground Reality

They looked absolutely devastated – the mother was in tears, wringing her hands and the father, he was too sullen to even speak coherently. Parents of a lady student, they had come down to see their hostel resident daughter. They hadn't heard from her for three weeks, no calls from her, nor any response to calls from them – no letters. In fact no news. They had panicked and rushed – is she all right?

Then, the mother looks for her in the hostel – the father waits outside. She comes back, terror stricken. Something is wrong, terribly wrong. Her room is locked. They rush to meet me – could you help. I was a senior faculty member – and had myself enquired from a hostelite or two, why the girl had suddenly become so irregular to class. Their classmates said, she was unwell – or that she'd gone home, and hurried on.

I sat the shivering couple and called two or three girls from the hostel, all seniors. I wanted answers. Where was this student? Why was her room locked?

A final year student whispers to me; she is in the room sir, only it is locked from outside. From outside? Locked in? How? Why?

Oh, this has been on for a few weeks now sir. Her room-mate has a strangle-hold on her, even her food is sent to the room. She has been kept captive – a prisoner – cut off from everyone else. We just stay away. It is bizarre. It all started when the duo always were together, even in the dining hall. Then, the pair preferred isolation, cutting off from everyone else, hardly ever leaving their room. Then it was only the senior, junior was forever inside, like bonded slave.

It was my turn to become speechless.

In twenty minutes, I was at the hostel door, and with the warden and matron, broke the lock and yanked the quivering girl out.

I took her aside to another room, and talked to her at length. It took her awhile to summon courage and open up. She looked tense, edgy and frightened. In fact she appeared wan and ghastly. Her narration of events leading to her total isolated, was to say least, shocking.

Why didn't she break out, confide in someone?

She stayed silent. So much like a mechanically operated robot. No expression, dead pan, un-animated.

A domineering, deviant female – and her docile, introverted and innocent junior roommate. To the horror of her parents, she took out her clothes from her cupboard, all ripped and torn, shredded. Her ear-rings and bangles, twisted and broken. On the skin of he forearms and back, incredibly, were a grid of linear streaks – razor blade tracks. She was black and blue in places, her spectacles, smashed. Her spirit was broken. She cowered like a cornered puppy, whimpering - psyched out totally. The psychological and physical violence this girl had borne was mind boggling.

While her mother sobbed uncontrollably, while the daughter sat impassive and stoic, oblivious to her presence.. That same day, the parents vacated the her from the hostel and took her home. She came back after six months of counseling, mental rehabilitation and physical recuperation. The senior girl was ejected from her room and mooring: she too went home, and returned after a few weeks.

Both continued their studies, uneventfully. The senior is now married and settled somewhere in the Gulf. The psyched and subjugated junior student is a fairly successful psychiatrist in a city. How deceptive looks and behavior are – it was tough to imagine that the simple salwar kameez clad cheerful senior was any way different from the others, yet in reality, she was – singularly devious. Why was the junior so subservient? I cannot figure out still: do dominated captive 'sex' slaves become victims of a form of Stockholm Syndrome?

It frightens me, of how much we expose our children and teenagers to in our pursuit of their education. How many suffer in silence, hating life, society and parents, scares me. Hostel life requires a strong bent of mind. Are children just out of ten plus two, brought up in the cozy comfort and security of home and family, mentally ready or prepared?

69

What's Age Got To Do With It

We are all happy for you, only that…
I've had enough of this but only this and only that
Okay, okay its your life, we wish you well, only
There you go again, with your ifs, buts and onlys.
Right then, here's wishing you all the best.

The problem is that I had finally found someone, after a long search, someone who vibes with me, complements my personality, not just hears me out, but listens too. The wait has been worth. The man is perfect. But, you know how it is, why him, why now---the endless rounds of inquisitive questions.

For me, it was enough we cared for each other. Being in love brought out so much in me I never knew even was within. His laughter is hearty and infectious, me too, me too – he says, squeezing my hands in his, looking into my eyes. My pulse races and I can hear my heart thud within its bony cage of ribs. I feel a quiver run down my spine – no, no matter what the world says – I have made up my mind. This is the man I want to be with, forever. Finis.

When he doesn't care a whit and I don't care a damn for the 'wide' gap in our ages, who the hell are others to comment on that difference. When two hearts throb in unison, time and tense are irrelevant.

My folks boycotted the marriage ceremony at the local registrar's office. His family, he knew would never come. A few friends of mine and a few of his and many of ours stood by as we signed the dotted lines. Some curious onlookers hung around the dour government office casting glances towards us, whispering.

Me, I was in my grandest silks. He was as usual, in his Wranglers. His jet black flaxen hair hung across his forehead and his rimless spectacles made him look natty. I hope I looked good too for this once in a lifetime occasion. A nagging worry though wormed its way into my brain – had I dyed my hair right? Were one or two streaks of white and grey still exposed? It does take time, this make up business. Camouflaging age is real hard work – harder still when you are forty two.

70

Her, Her Husband and His Best Friend

It made her uncomfortable: the way he looked askance, at her, every now and then, especially when his colleagues and friends dropped by. The eyes, they seemed to gore into her very being. Was she imagining, she hoped she was. Yet, deep inside of her she felt edgy – the looks were pretty 'loaded'. With questions, with queries. Was her husband getting ideas? Was he suspecting something was going on between her and his best friend? He was stupid to even entertain such thoughts. Yet, she felt herself squirming on the sofa as she sat with her husband and his pal, chatting, laughing and enjoying the weekend.

She had heard of overtly possessive types, spouses who suspected every move, attributed ulterior motives to every relationship – doubted every male around was trying to make passes or advances towards their partners. Monitored every phone call and opened every letter – wanted to know the content (or intent) of every e-mail or e-mailer. Chaperoning their wives even for routine vegetable market outings – accompanying them for sari buying or to the blouse stitching tailor –

He wasn't like that, this guy: but, somewhere in the recent past, she had started to be made uncomfortable whenever his friend visited. He tried his best to send her away, get us coffee please – oho, a little hotter please – ouch – not that hot – ooh, too much sugar – each time she had to return to the kitchen to undo or do damage control. Surely, it was now getting obvious to her – her husband was suspecting her.

She made a decision, she'd keep off. She'd find work in the kitchen to keep her engaged – and away – maybe chat with her friends on phone, write, watch TV – anything to avoid the icy looks and accusatory glances. She wasn't guilty of anything, neither had he ever voiced or hinted about anything. It was just the way he looked at her, that said it all. Was she imagining things? No, no, she was certain – this was for real. Unsaid, understood.

She left the two friends to themselves from then on. She made them tea and called her hubby over to the kitchen to hand over the tray – pretending to be too busy with cooking to leave the kitchen. The charade brought peace, peace of mind to her: she didn't have to withstand the constant 'being watched' sensation.

She was never that type: nor ever was. Again and again the questions on why rankled and agitated her mind. What was it that her husband had noticed or seen that made him feel this way. Could there be some basis, some other clue, as to why her loving spouse felt threatened? She watched the buddies.

She had gently shifted the curtain of the kitchen door and looked at the two men in animated conversation, debating the merits or otherwise of the third umpire's run-out decision. She saw his visiting colleague look up and past her husband's shoulder, right towards her standing and peeping from behind the half closed curtain. He caught her eye, and winked. Winked, not blinked.

She was too stunned: such brazenness - such betrayal. She hated him – to what she had done to her – demeaned her status. His best friend's wife. Then rage built up. Infernal anger, at how, she, not the rogue was paying the penalty, under the scanner all day. How could that man, or this man treat her like this? Obviously her husband was too scared or nervous about his friend's overt advances – perhaps he had seen signs, and his whole approach was not in telling that guy off, but in pushing her, the innocent one in purdah. Men, bah @*&#%$@&

The friend's secret wink had not gone unnoticed by her man – slowly, he turned backwards, and saw her standing at the kitchen door, behind the curtain. All events were unfolding in a trice. Slow motion, rapid action. The wink, the swivel, her peep – than something snapped in her – no, this isn't fair, she who had such faith and trust in her husband was now in constrained to prove her loyalty everyday from the dock for no fault of hers –

Then in full view of the two men, she did something she never thought she could – slowly and deliberately, she pushed the curtain wider, and winked – at the visitor. It takes a palm to slap, and two to pummel - her calculated signal disconcerted and rattled the men. The friend was taken aback, how could this woman wink in full view of her man, even though I.... and her husband, he was nonplussed too - did his wife wink at his friend, or him? He would never know - rather, he wouldn't want to find an answer to that question. It might be one he didn't want to hear.

In less than two minutes she sees her chastened husband escort an embarrassed colleague out of her home. No, he didn't dare ask her anything. She had taught both men a lesson, they'd remember for life. Corner a kitten and you turn it into a tigress. A man - eating tigress.

71

One-Way Romance

Anyone with minimum common sense could infer – that Royal Enfield bullet 350cc was a bit too huge for him,. He, a medical hostel friend of ours, was a diminutive simpleton from Andhra. He wasn't too comfortable with English. The inability to communicate saw him stick to a select few. Son, the only son, of a rich mine owner he was heir to a minor fortune.

He was head over heels with a female in his class. She, a heavily stacked top-heavy Tamil lass with an infectious smile. A chatterbox if ever there was one, she was quite popular – popular enough to get unanimously elected as the class representative, a rare event, for girls never ever stood for union slots or got elected in those days.

She walked like a plump hen, her twin prows scything the air in front of her. Now, Nayana, she wasn't even aware of her secret admirer. He pined and moaned – in teen parlance, it was 'one way traffic'. He didn't have the guts to blurt out to her, or even face her. All he did was plaster his room wall with tiny pics of hers (snipped off from the college magazine), with the slogan 'I love you' painted in color beneath every picture. He breathed, talked and dreamt Nayana. He had a spool tape recorder that eternally belted out some depressing guttural Telugu number or other crooned by Ghantashaala or duets by A M Raja and Jikki.

But Nayana, she had other admirers, more dashing than our bumbling Babu. Truth be said, the flock of boys that trailed her, was in part, I suspect, more because of her ample top-storey anatomical twin assets than her anything else. It is a known anthropological fact, right from pre-historical epochs, men have a fixation for mammary volume – obviously that gene persists to modern times.

So Babu would moon and drive his Enfield in circles on the basketball court in the hostel (after someone bigger got his bike off its stand, kick started it and helped the jockey sized rider astraddle). Hours on end, bike and Babu went round and round, with an occasional high pitched horn toot toot to shoo away a lazy cow or two that sauntered into his endless orbit.

Come December, Nayana left for home, enroute, on the Westcoast Express, we learnt she'd developed severe abdominal craps. She was rushed to a private nursing home straight from the Madras Central by her parents – and sad to mention, she never recovered from an anesthetic mishap that followed an uneventful surgery for acute appendicitis.

Babu was never the same again. His bike stood untouched and rusted in the humid Mangalore weather. He himself withered and shriveled and became completely introverted. He ate alone and stayed put in his shut room for days on end. In short, he was turning loony. His parents, who were informed by the authorities of the mental status of their son, came and took him away. We later heard, he had become stark insane and had to be institutionalized.

For years after these events, the once gleaming Royal Enfield stood in the hostel corridor, abandoned. It was still standing when I vacated the place after I completed my course.

A few evenings ago, the TV playing "uravum illai, pagayum illai – onrummey illai…." An eternally popular sure-fire tear jerker from the blockbuster of yore, Devadas. I stood silent and closed my eyes, my thoughts and memories floating back to far off days in the seventies.

Into my mind's misty ken appear images – of Babu's bike and it's endless spirals, of his unrequited romance, of Nayana and her toothy smile and overburdened endowments and her unfortunate tragic death. I also the image of a once simple friend, become a manic depressive patient, strapped to his steel cot in a forsaken mental asylum.

I took the TV remote and pressed the mute button.

If only I was built a little stronger mentally or gifted with less powerful memory powers, I'd have let the dirge play on……I like that song, but the package of rattling memories it comes with, haunts.

72

Sweethearts & Schools

The list was impressive and was painted in bright red. Right at the entrance of the school. The Ten Commandments......Thou shalt not do this, do that or anything else enjoyable for that matter. A grim early morning reminder to the teens that trooped in, watch your step pal, Big Brother watches......the lost of don'ts (there was no list of dos or can try) zoomed in and out of my mind, awake or asleep. Being educated in convent schools run by nuns or fathers had the effect of making everyone feel a sinner.

Can I have a second helping of those delicious idlis?

Just as the bowl steaming puffed white flat snowballs are shoved towards me...I dither.......gluttony...oops, that's a sin too. Reluctantly I avert my eyes. Who wants to stand in a line on bent knees hearing the creator tick off your trespasses someday: irresistible? Go ahead, pop that jignut jaggery ball into your 'gob'. Who knows with so many doing the same, one never knows even the all-seeing eye may miss one small boy's sleight of hand. The commandments even made one munch or chew with minimum mandibular movement. Easy, easy. Actually, more than God, we, at that age, feared Fr. Di Fiore's eye. It caught everything. We shivered in our half pants, if this man of the cloth had such an eagle sight what can one say about the one he lives his life for?

Add to this collective guilt that we all carried in our daily lives, being marched off to the chapel for confession and singing psalms and hymns truly made us feel like prodigal children. Page 36, the father would announce and we flipped the hymn book and joined his hi pitched vice to chorus off key, "Follow, follow, I will follow Jesus, anywhere, everywhere I will follow on" or "Rolled away, rolled away, rolled away, every burden of my heart rolled away" and such.

And it was not just gluttony, or lying or thieving that really frightened the daylights out of us – it was the presence of girls. The school was co-educational, and a good smattering of skirts was in every classroom. We did everything to stay away from them, try as we might though, I must admit some stray 'impious' ideas and scenarios did flit across our adolescent hearts. We shook ourselves quick, a splash of water from the row of taps in the corridor brought our thinking process back to admissible levels of piety. We were too young to understand the import of 'Thou shalt not commit adultery'. Only much later did we learn that winking one's eye or blowing a kiss were not, per definition adulterous acts that would one day see us fry in purgatory.

But who or what can deter any boy from making advances. Most did. And the little ladies were no nuns either, in fact they usually winked first. A host of clandestine hush hush affairs were on any given time, sufficient enough proof of the goings-on was found liberally etched by Cupid stricken of their under the desk romance on the desk tops for posterity. Love as we all know, knows no barriers, and not too surprisingly, Eros struck Subbu.

Subramaniam had impressive initials that preceded his name. K. S, for Kalavai Sreenivasa. A dyed in the wool Tamil Brahmin of Iyer stock he started and ended his days with recitation of slokas, extolling the rising or setting sun. A broad triple stripe of vibhuti (holy ash) ran across his broad forehead. On special days, like for geometry tests, the middle line of the three ashen tracks bore a red vermillion impression – and he had a unique way of reeling out the rahu kalam of the day by tap-counting his knuckles and their in-between depressions – oh, today Tuesday, it is bad times between this O Clock to that O Clock. Frankly he was a misfit in this crowd of drainpipe pants and side-burned anglos.

Now Subramaniam, had the hots for Ruth, and vice versa. Ruth, whose mummy was a teacher in Rosary Matric, was a petite pretty doll. She was special too, in that, she was the only one permitted to take Latin as her second language. Yes, not Hindi like us hoi polloi chose, not Tamil like some opted for, or French like a few took, but LATIN. Gosh, was she something! This lissome latino. And Subbu was besotted good. Rumor had it she sent him love chits in Latin, and who else, but the H-Iyer High Q Mylapore suitor knew a few appropriate terms in that language, especially ones that concerned romance.

All was fine, the budding romance bloomed – except that in the school mess Subbu sat quite far from others, his brahminical unidimensional menu packed with much maternal concern by his amma – nicely soured curd-rice with a twist of dehydrated 'naarthanga' pickle packed in a flat stainless steel tiffin box – and his rigorous upbringing made him squat apart – he couldn't stand the smell of fish or the sight of pork chops or chicken legs. That stuff made him retch and choke.

Now pardon me mentioning this, but it was my observation that the way Subbu used the spoon was unique. He would scoop a heap of saadam and 'a la Rajni cigarette trick', flip it into his mouth. This peculiar method of using the spoon to transfer stuff I find is quite common among Brahmins. The spoon is held like a toothbrush with handle pointing inwards, the rice is spaded out, and in one rapid upward flip, the distal end of the upside down spoon with its contents is right inside the eater's mouth – the spoon is never brought head end in, but head end out and over. The physics involved in the maneuver is mind boggling – imagine the amount of centripetal / centrifugal forces involved in keeping that quivering spoonful of thayir saadam in place, right throughout its circular arc and the tangential force needed to dislodge it at the precise moment. Anyway, this blog is deviating, so back to Ruth and romance.

One of the unwritten, but well known commandments that bound boyfriends to their heartthrobs, here in this school was, exchange of – believe it or not – spit. The lady love had to spit out a gob of gooey saliva into the boy's palm and he did likewise into hers: then to seal their mutual fondness to eternity – each had to swallow the other's spit.

When the more senior green with jealousy boys got wind of the proportions the Subbu Ruth dalliance was taking, they put their foot down. The side – burn sporting boys, cornered Ruth and Subbu during the luncheon recess and coerced them to declare and seal their evermore evergreen allegiance with the spit swap ritual.

Watched by dozens, Ruth swallowed Subbu's yoghurt flavored spit – and Subbu, he didn't even extend his palm, let alone ingest Ruth's parotid gland secretion. Its off, the referees declared. Subbu is a rat they murmured in unison and Ruth, the poor thing…., she was bathed in sighs, sobs and secretions from another pair of glands, the lachrymals.

73

The sexy silver-screen siren

Might as well meet up with this guy I thought. He'd been calling ever since he heard I was in city. Dying to meet up with me, this buddy of mine was, a fellow professional. A 'doctor', an incomplete one, actually. He never completed the course. We had studied together, me going on to take up teaching and he foraying into the wide world to make his pile.

The half doc thought deep....never mind the degree, who cares...just put a board, call yourself a doc...and stick to the safest procedures. Skin, is really the largest organ in the human body: that said, it is clear it must be site for most afflictions, mostly harmless ones. Rash, itch and such like. Once a skin patient, always a skin patient. There are no permanent cures: some drugs work bringing dramatic relief and change…but alas, for the patient that is, the condition returns and it is back to the doc. And mind you, skin docs treat sexually transmitted diseases too and that means more moola. Moreover, as such patient wants to be seen hanging round in a consultant's chamber. The plaintive plea is always please doc, check me, but at my place…. The skin-fellow just hops over there, jabs a syringe or two in secret and collects a wad or two of crisp notes for his hush-hush tryst and laughs all the way to the bank (twice a day, actually).

So this good for nothing classmate of mine carefully weighed the supply-demand dynamics and incognito income to opt to 'specialize' in skin. The over-riding factor of course was that dermatology presented no emergencies. Regular 9 to 5 job, cushy really. As far as I knew the friend of mine was a big cipher in clinical knowledge and I often wondered how he got along: he knew just one or two skin problems, at most.

I hadn't met him for years, so it would be nice to catch up with stuff and maybe chuckle over a few adventures of old, mimic a professor or two….and exchange notes on who where, with who, doing what.

I'd heard that this phony guy got hitched to a film actress. He wed the sultry siren screen Goddess. News media was flush with the snaps on the 'made for each other couple'. For me it was a huge mystery. How come this 'also ran' from a middle class run of the mill family with no pretension to estate or elitism, met with and married the tinsel-town queen?

He picked me up in a chauffeur driven swanky limo: We eased into a massive mansion, bedecked to its gills. Hmm, this is how stars dwell eh! Cool, I mused.

Once in, we got down to chatting, filling in the blanks and gaps. Inevitably, the topic veered round to matrimony and family, whence, anticipating my query 'how come all this?' he laughed loud, proceeding to brief me on how it all began and ended up like this. May be its best I put it as he said it, as a first person account, in his own words.

......Well, you know I had no option but to open shop. Life was hard and running a clinic with borrowed capital was arduous. Anyway, just a few weeks into my practice as I rode to my practice on my second-hand scooter, I spotted a Mercedes Benz parked nearby. No sooner had I stepped in, I saw a uniformed driver smartly salute me asking me if I was the doctor. In ten minutes I was in the plush air-con Merc reeking of perfume, being driven to a palatial place in the outskirts of the city.

Waiting for me was the silver screen diva herself. She quickly ushered me into her private room, where she broke down and sobbed. In a nutshell, she had developed a skin condition that was psyching her out.

Please doc, help me...my career is ruined if this thing gets out.

I chuckled to myself, for here was the sexy siren, famed for turning them on with her oomph, who waxed eloquently on TV ads 'The secret of my glowing skin, LUX', now weeping uncontrollably over her skin problem.

She sobbed, Oh, doctor, I am so petrified. Is it serious?

I quickly sized up the 'made made for me' situation

Could become serious if left untreated any longer, may even lead to acute glomerulo-nephritis

Glom...er... what?

Kidney failure.

Good God! Please do something doc and fast, she buried her pretty face in her palms and wailed.

I didn't take me long to decide on my plan of action: my modus operandi. Neat and simple and tailor made too.

Then without any further delay, you will need to moisten her whole body (except face and head) with a specially medicated emulsion I will send over.

But doc, I am so terrified…could you help me…..uh medicate me? And pleeease no one should know about all this...puleeeese

Lets see....you've contracted scabies

That's how I ended up dabbing the harmless formulation benzyl benzoate all over every inch and voluptuous curve of hers, asking her to shower herself after an hour. Twice more during the next few days I repeated the 'anointing', I myself scrubbing in her marble bath tub on the last occasion. For effect, I used my surgical gloves before proceeding, reminding her, of how this affliction was quite often 'sexually transmitted and always a highly contagious one' (for shock effect of course). Though she reddened and blushed, I knew she was scared out of her wits. One thing led to another… In a month, I found myself exchanging garlands. That's the whole story pal, of how I am like "this and here" –

He rolled his eyes and waved his hands around like an umpire signalling a '20-20 free hit'.

Boy! That was good one! I couldn't but help smiling. How dame fortune favors a chosen one. Strange isn't it that sarcoptis scabies a microscopic skin parasite helped you find your female, fame and fortune eh? I asked incredulously.

'Scabies? What scabies?' Ha ha ha….he says, nudging my ribs with his elbow, winking as he leaned over, dropping his voice to a whisper … 'To tell the truth, she didn't have any infection. Just a mild reaction to a mosquito's bite'………….

All along my drive back to the hotel room I ruminated over the story I'd just heard. What a cad? What a second rate scoundrel. What an unethical scalawag……

Yet, I must admit a very, very smart one……

74

A Damsel In Distress

Just as I with my wife and daughter were leaving the restaurant after dinner, I saw this burka clad female almost tripping over as she dashed across some tables to me. Please sir, she says, amid panting breaths, save me. I had no clue as to what this was all about. Almost the entire crowd in the restaurant, I notice, has its head turned towards us.

Excuse me, who is this? I say, stepping back. I'm Meher sir, your student. Meher? Meherunisa? She looked so different. Suddenly seeing her in a flowing black veiled burkha, instead of her usual salwar kameez made her so alien.

See sir, just look beyond my shoulders, there at that last corner table- you see sir, those are some relatives from Bombay – and they want to fix me up with tat guy with them. My parents too are here, nodding agreement. Please sir, stop this. Sir, I do not want marriage now sir.

By now, the place was agog, and I saw one or two walk towards me, menacingly. Okay, listen Meher, just meet me in the college before eight. I'll wait there. We can't talk here.

No sir, not tomorrow, can't you talk to these people now?

Tomorrow, eight.

One, much fuming man, her father possibly, grabbed her by her shoulders and led her back. The entire episode maybe lasted just three minutes or less. The restaurant was managed by a Muslim and was heavily patronized by local Muslim families. The scene was almost like from out of a movie. My wife was too shocked, and my daughter, she holds on to my arm tight. Lets go from here.

I quickly exited. Next morning I was in the college porch early. I saw her being dropped in a fiat car by someone. I walked towards her as she entered the gate. She saw me and rushed forwards, and then I saw, someone get down from the car, run in and to my utter amazement, he pounced on the frail girl and started beating her to pulp. She was on the ground and he kicked her quite savagely uttering four letter words. What riled the man, her father, I was certain by now, is that I was giving her a ear and that she had sought help to extricate herself from matrimonial compulsions. He glared at me when I tried to intervene.

She's my daughter you bastard. Just keep off.

Though I am by nature a non-violent person, some overpowering urge took over and I myself was surprised with my physical strength – I pushed the man, quite sturdy - yanked Meher back to her feet – and screamed...

One more move and you're dead mister. She maybe your daughter at home, but here, she's my student and anyone troubles any student of mine will pay for it.

I was boiling with rage. By now, a few others in the campus came over, and they warned the man to get out of the premises. The girl herself was too shocked, and with a bleeding nose. I took her inside the college and calmed her down. Many more girls, who by now had arrived, stood by her and promised all help.

Now, I was real worried. What next? Meher was terrified, her dad would kill her if she went home. Her mother cannot be counted on, as she was as scared. What started off as a simple case for sage advise had now turned into a mammoth dilemma. That evening, after class, I took Meher home; mine – and the next day, with some help from the institution head, I moved her into the ladies hostel: the administration was sympathetic and allowed time for handling the issue.

I with two other colleagues met and decided to chip in and pool resources. We paid her dues, bought her personal effects – and she continued in the course, despite periodic threats and ultimatums from her dad. In a year, her mother and sister sent her help clandestinely. Over the next few terms, she coped well, academically, and passed her finals creditably.

Meher took a transfer to Bangalore for her 12 month internship, away from her people. She got a merit admission into dermatology, post-graduating with a Diploma. She rang me up telling me if Nepal was a good place for work. I said yes, being far away from Mangalore was her best option: her father was quite powerful, and he had even met my employers asking for my transfer for interfering in family affairs. Fortunately, nothing adverse happened. In fact, because of my firm stand and support in this case, I had become some sort of knight, for I was approached by one or two other girl students to intercede on their behalf and parley with bull-headed parents or relatives.

A few years ago, I found out from local newspapers that her father, a building contractor, had passed away. When I last heard, Meher was still single. I wonder where she is now or what has become of her. I haven't heard from her for eleven years now.

75

Sex Appeal

I am tired of being plain looking. Staid, sober, serious. That's how everyone knows me. That's how I know myself. No one even notices me. No second looks. I coalesce into crowds and merge with the background. Nothing distinguishes me. Okay, alright, I have some a couple of hi end academic achievements, but so have many. Just look at me. Grey sari, oiled plait, dark complexion and spectacles to boot. Ughs! I screamed silently as I turn away from the mirror. I am pathetic. My face sank into my palms as sobs shook my shoulders. Life had passed me by. I am at thirty one still unnoticed, un-wooed, unwed and unhappy.

This is routine, this self pity and regret at what life had given me. A raw deal, that's for sure. I slowly packed my suitcase; I had to attend a conference on cell membrane biology at Hyderabad. My research paper on some recent advances and work done in my lab had been accepted for presentation. Not that it said anything seminal. This was a mish-mashed recycled paper and had nothing new to say. But that's what seminars and workshops are about. Travel allowance, liberal grants, ritzy hotels. Who but a fool would miss these perks? Not me: these were the only avenues of change for me. The dash to the airport, the flight, the arrival, the moving into a fancy star hotel. So many times, so often, the same rigmarole. My life really is a bore. Robotic. Mechanical.

Early next day, I freshened up and for once used an impressive looking free sachet of shampoo the hotel bath had a collection of. I let my hair loose and on a whim, walked into the beauty parlour near the foyer. Two hours later, and I looked and felt alien. Eye brows, facial, waxing, the works. The indulgence was worth the scalping cost. I returned to my room and changed. On a whim I wrapped the simmering coal black sari that had been lying with me for months, unused. Too sheer and see through. I shoved the waistline of the petticoat down a few inches, the sari dipping to dangerous territory down my belly. Hipster eh!

Let me give it a go, I smiled. Who cares what I do. I picked up the black lacy bra, two sizes too tight for me anyway and struggled into its fit. My sleeveless low neck cleavage peeping blouse made me feel like a vamp. But what the heck! This Hyderabad was new to me: no one except a few senior, straight-laced and staid academicians. All rapt in their cocooned world of labs and cell structure. Nerds. Eggheads. Geeks.

I sashayed onto the rostrum for my presentation. Then I felt it, an intense, being 'stared at' feeling: everyone was gaping at me. I was being mentally stripped. I felt a tingle. I let my pallu slip (accidentally, I promise) to expose a black strap as I pinned the collar microphone, flashed a radiant good morning and poured my stuff out. The oohs and aahs my slide show and delivery was interrupted with, wasn't for the paper content – it was for the oomph I chose to exude in oodles. I was astounded at the electric reaction: the assembly actually rose in unison and clapped, long and loud. At lunch I giggled coquettishly as I was mobbed, jostled, pinched, groped.

I excused myself and rushed to the ladies room. I stared at the wall to wall mirror and shook myself. Was this me? A few strips of black-straps on my bare shoulder, a few inches of waist skin and an exposed belly button: sleeveless, haloed mane, mascara, eye shadow, eyeliner, mascara, rouge, lip gloss…The delegates. They didn't observe, they ogled. They didn't see, they gawked. They didn't listen, they drooled. Men.... scums....slimeballs. And to the ladies here……boo to you too. I smirked inwardly as I watched them squirm uneasily in their plush conference hall chairs.

Now I know what the world laps up and warms to. Not brains, not charm, not honesty; its plain sex appeal. That turns heads and churns the underbelly ……. ask Silk Smitha, ask Protima Bedi ask Rekha…ask Tina Turner, ask Halle Berry……ask the starlet who wants to make it big on the silver screen, if she'd strip for the camera: 'I will, if the script demands it' she chirps. Or ask me.

I have prepaid invitations to four more conferences this year, all shoved into my manicured fingers and palm by frustrated paws. My mobile hasn't stopped tinkling. It doesn't pay to be single and simple, one needs to be single and sexy. If oozing oomph is the new paradigm for popularity, then I will ooze – and ooze it in oodles.

The script demands it.

76

Campus Capers

After a full day's work, it was nice to be back, home: a warm shower and a bit of unwinding – perfect recipe for revival of spirits – or so I thought. A call got me hurrying back to my office. A 2nd year boy and girl had been caught, pants and panties down: They were confronted in an empty lecture hall in a 'compromising position' (those were the words used by the security officer who stumbled on the duo). Being a former cop, he was quite thorough and professional (to a fault often) in discharge of his duties.

He spotted an open window in the basement lecture hall and stealthily crept down the corridor, peeped over the ledge and filmed the 'roll in the hay' on his mobile before he busted the sheepish 'lovers'.

It was not pleasant experience for me: the finesse required in handling delicate matters like this was not my forte. Anyway, after roundly ticking off the students, I asked them to bring their parents to my office within twenty-four hours. What they had been doing wasn't something anyone would be proud of. It was despicable and disgraceful (I chose polite adjectives, despite my growing rage).

The girl sobbed and booed uncontrollably and the boy stood wringing his hands wearing a woebegone expression.

I was sure, within the hour, the hot news would be staple gossip fare in the campus, but by the next day, I could lid the affair by asking the parents to take the culprits home (separately, if you please) for a week or two. Of course I would take some drastic punitive action later, as the issue was grave and invited penalty.

When I returned home, I got news that someone high up in the management hierarchy had was trying to contact me desperately: when I got to him, he spoke more like a devastated parent than an aggrieved administrator. He counseled patience and asked me to drop the whole issue: close the case. I fumbled for words as I was quite livid, but, when the voice at the other end asked me 'what would you do doctor if your daughter was the one caught?

'Deal with the matter in a dignified and decorous mien; Do not, no matter what, do anything that will besmirch the girl's life permanently and indelibly for life'.

It took a good hour for me to gather my senses and sanity. Yes, I was overreacting. The students could well have been our children. How would we want them to be treated? Like criminals or like adolescents gone astray?

The next morning I informed the pair accused to leave their parents out of the imbroglio. They were individually sent for counseling. It is now many years since the incident took place. Both the erring teens are now decent medical professionals (married, not to each other) and doing well.